An
Ambulance
Is
on
the
Way

Also by Jonathan Wilson

FICTION

A Palestine Affair

The Hiding Room

Schoom

CRITICISM

Herzog

On Bellow's Planet:
Readings from the Dark Side

An Ambulance Is on the Way

Stories of Men in Trouble

Jonathan Wilson

Pantheon Books
New York

Pantheon Books and colophon are registered trademarks of
Random House, Inc.

Some of the stories in this collection were previously
published in the following:

"After Love" and "Tosh" in *The Jewish Quarterly*
"Last Light" in *NIT*
"Mini-Joe" in *New Writing* 9
"Mother with Child" in *The New Yorker*
"Dead Ringers" in *The Slow Mirror: New Fiction by Jewish
    Writers* (Five Leaves Publications, Nottingham,
    England, 1996)

Library of Congress Cataloging-in-Publication Data
Wilson, Jonathan, (date).
An ambulance is on the way : stories of men in trouble /
Jonathan Wilson.
p.   cm.
ISBN 0-375-42210-2
1. Middle-aged men—Fiction.   2. Conduct of life—
Fiction.   3. Humorous stories, English.   I. Title.
PR6073.I4679A83   2005
823'.914—dc22   2004052051

www.pantheonbooks.com
Book design by Virginia Tan
Printed in the United States of America
First Edition
9 8 7 6 5 4 3 2 1

For Adam
and Gabriel

Night nurse, the pain is
getting worse.

—*Gregory Isaacs*

Contents

An
Ambulance
Is
on
the
Way

Sons
of
God

"All this," said Wayne the plumber, "was written down in the Bible five thousand years ago." He was out on the deck, taking a break from doing angioplasty on the pipes beneath my kitchen sink. Meanwhile, he was giving his assistant, John Pickles, a lesson.

"Hey, Wayne," I yelled from an upstairs window, "you're wrong about the date. Most of the events in the Bible didn't even take place five thousand years ago. Solomon, for example, in all his glory, at best got going about three thousand years ago, and nobody wrote the diary of his activities until at least a century later."

I shouldn't have gotten involved. But why not? I was desperate to get in on a theological discussion, especially with Wayne. Wayne was a plumber all right, but he was also a missionary in Ecuador. He returned to the States one year out of every five and ran the roads from North Carolina to Boston, replacing and repairing the broken and burst pipes of the bourgeoisie. After that it was back to church in the poor places outside Quito, where conversion was his calling.

"Be that as it may," Wayne shouted back, "I'd have to see some evidence."

Ah, evidence! I hadn't been subscribing to *Biblical Archaeological Review* for nothing—although it was almost nothing given the generous terms of their initial subscription rate. But evidence is a paltry thing compared to passion, and this, I knew, was where Wayne would have me by the U bolt.

It, and by *it* I mean my desperation, had begun quietly enough on a soft summer day in the first year of the new millennium C.E. (I'm being careful here). The traffic on Route 9 outside the Chestnut Hill Mall congested and fumed, but the SUV in front of me presented a hopeful bumper sticker very much in favor of Jesus. It had been a long time since I had really thought about Jesus. In all likelihood, in the way of my people in the few but noisy and concentrated places that we occupied in the vast world, I had never given him a fair shake.

So I shook. In the historical, evidentiary direction, of course. It turned out, discovered on my excursion to the Newton Public Library section 801.3, that Jesus wasn't just Jewish, he was *really* Jewish. Not only did he have no idea he was a Christian; he never imagined that he might become one. In addition, if I could work up the courage, I had some news to break to Wayne,

4

and it was earth-shattering. According to the two most eminent professors of Jewish Jesus, "son of God" was an Aramaic figure of speech. Digest that! It meant nothing more and nothing less than "pious dude." It wasn't at all uncommon on the dusty streets outside Jerusalem for young studs to greet one another in the swish tongue of the day, with a friendly "Hey, son of God, how you doing?"

Now, I had known for some time how dangerous inspired language could be to the literal-minded. For example, my own lot, the Jews. Who told us to strap a little black box with a prayer inside onto our heads once a day? Answer: no one. "And ye shall bind these words upon your forehead" clearly meant "remember them." But no, a hundred years pass and someone dreams up the apparatus. Soon enough he's got a business going, and the leather guy is happy, so who wants to interfere with at least two men's livelihoods?

I was trying not to interfere with Wayne's, but there was no turning back. After a quick refresher read-up in *The Changing Face of Jesus* by Gezer Vermes, pages 12 to 25, I went down into the kitchen.

"OK," I said, "how do you explain this? The Book of John says that the Last Supper took place on the day *before* the Passover Seder, but the Synoptic Gospels— that's Matthew, Mark, and Luke . . ."

"Yes, I know what they are," Wayne said. He was patient with me.

"Well, they date it on the day *of* the Seder. You see what I'm saying. They can't both be right."

Wayne had his head under the sink. His legs were sticking out.

"John—" He was trying hard to project his voice, but I lost the rest of his sentence.

"It's impossible, you see," I continued, "that the Jews could have held a court hearing the following day, on Passover itself. That was against the rules. So John must have got it wrong."

Wayne slid his pear-shaped body out from under the sink. His blond hair was flattened. He looked a little like Yogi Bear.

"'The rules'? 'Impossible'?"

"Yes."

"Well, didn't you ever hear of rules being broken?"

He had a point there. I had to admit that it was really hard to know what had gone down between pink dawn and rosy dusk on consecutive days two thousand years ago. I'd probably have to go back to the library.

"All I know," Wayne said, "is that we could do with someone like Jesus now."

He stood up. He was a head taller than I was, and he had a wrench in his hand.

I decided to leave the "son of God" issue until after he'd fixed the pipes.

Wayne dropped the wrench into his toolbox. "Are you," he asked, "by any chance a connoisseur of the ancient languages?"

"I know a little Italian," I replied.

"The Hebrew aleph," he went on, "is a pictorial

symbol of the shift from a hunting to an agrarian cul-
ture. The letter is made up of a bull's horns and a broken ring. The taming of the bull, you see. There is a
bull in a paddock not far from my house in the village
of Pifo who has a brass ring in his nose. I call him
Aleph."

"That's fascinating," I said. "So you don't believe
that Hebrew is a holy tongue."

"I believe in the holy tongue of fire that is Our Lord
Jesus Christ."

"When do you think you'll be done with the sink?"
I asked.

"This job," Wayne said, "is quite complicated. It
looks as if someone has been shoving Q-tips and rice
down the waste disposal. It could take all day to
unblock."

It was dinnertime. My wife, Claire, and I were eating
pad Thai ordered in from Take-Out Taxi. My son, Nick,
had his own hamster food, three lettuce leaves and
a crouton. He was starving himself in order to make
weight for his first varsity high school wrestling match.

"Did you know," I began, "that the aleph is a pictorial symbol . . ."

"Wayne been round again?" my wife interrupted.
"I thought he was back in Ecuador."

"Next month. He returns next month."

"Maybe you should go with him."

She had been harsh with me for two days—since she had overheard me on the phone telling a friend that I was in love with Helen Hunt. At the time she'd gotten off a scathing "Yeah, like she's gonna call *you*." I thought that was the end of the matter, but it turned out to be just the beginning.

My son looked up from his leaves.

"*Temptation Island* tonight," he said.

"Disgusting," my wife responded. "You're just like your father. And don't you watch anything other than Fox?"

"Yes," he replied, "I watch *Cribs* and sometimes there's stuff on the WB."

I was thinking hard about the historical Jesus, but as I'd already bombed with the aleph I didn't want to broach the subject in conversation.

The festival of Hanukkah was approaching, with its lovely candle lights not to be used for utilitarian purposes. I could have mentioned this at the dinner table, but that was to risk sounding like a religious fanatic, when in fact I was merely a sentimentalist and eclectic reader with too much time on his hands. Wrestling seemed safe.

"What weight are you going at?" I asked Nick.

"One seventy."

"And what do you weigh now?"

"One seventy-five."

He had the crouton speared on the end of his fork.

"Don't you think," he said, "that your friend Paul Vogel looks exactly like Osama bin Laden?"

It was true, but Paul Vogel also looked like Kobe Bryant and Scottie Pippen. And a little kid in New York City had once approached him on a bus and asked if he was Jesus.

I reminded everybody of this, and then I ate the shrimp out of the pad Thai while avoiding the noodles.

"According to the most unimpeachable sources," I ventured, "Jesus was probably a Galilean Hasid, a pious wanderer, a miracle worker from out of the cold north."

There was silence in the room. Only the fridge muttered something in reply, buzzed up, probably, by my Nordic reference.

Eventually Claire said: "I'm sure it's hot in the Galilee, most of the time, anyway."

I'd expected this blow to fall, but anticipation didn't help to reduce its impact. These were serious times, and there was no excuse at all for flights of fancy in the service of a decent sentence.

"Are you going to come and watch?" Nick asked.

"When's the meet?"

"Wednesday night."

"I'll be there," I said.

It wasn't as if I had anything else to do. I was recuperating from a laparoscopy performed one week earlier to remove my rebellious gallbladder, which had decided to swell to the bursting point and then spit tiny stones into the narrow channel that rushed deliveries to my liver, creating a blockage that not even Wayne could have foreseen.

The phone rang.

"You get it," my wife said.

It was Paul Vogel calling from San Francisco.

"Hey," I said, "we were just talking about you. The uncanny resemblance."

"Tell me about it," he replied. "I can't go out of the house. Half the neighborhood thinks I want to blow up the Golden Gate Bridge."

"Did you think about shaving off your beard?"

"What are you, the Taliban? This is a free country. You can micromanage your own facial hair."

"You're right," I said. "That's the beauty of America."

We talked for a while about my scar, which was less a scar than four little holes deftly drilled by Dr. Pamela Gevertz, who was thirty and a newlywed.

"They pulled the gangrenous gallbladder out through my navel," I said.

"Helen might like to know that," my wife put in without looking up from her plate.

The crowd around the wrestling mat was standing-room only. The bout in progress offered an uncontroversial intergender affair, for these are open prairie days in the wide United States such as the world has never known. A boy in the 190-pound range had spread his arms to circle the girth of his female twin. As the view cleared before me he threw her to the ground and began to twist her arm. Somehow, Atlas rose, lifted her rival up on her back, and shunted him all the way to the perimeter. "Good job, Teresa!" the man next to me shouted. He was wearing a T-shirt that had the words *Hombres de Acero* printed above the yellow and black logo of the Pittsburgh Steelers. Teresa's parents, her teammates, their parents, and all the women in the audience from our side cheered wildly. The wrestlers untangled, returned to the middle of the circle, and began to grab at each other again.

"It's like watching a marriage, isn't it?" said a skinny dad on my left whom I knew to be a recent divorcé.

"Or Jacob wrestling with the angel," I responded, but my interlocutor pretended that he hadn't heard me and I looked away as if I hadn't spoken.

OK, so it wasn't only Jesus. Thoughts on religious matters were leeching onto my brain at an appalling rate, and this had been the case ever since my early dismissal from the hospital on the dual grounds of my body's good behavior and pressure from managed care.

I lie. The trouble had begun even earlier, in the brown, unhappy hour before surgery. There I was, half asleep in the arms of Morpheus, when my long-dead father stretched out his arm and clapped a silky yarmulke onto the back of my head. I was deeply grateful—glad, in a worst-case scenario—to meet my maker in the proper attire. Ten minutes later I was less appreciative when Norma, my still-living mother-in-law, showed up in the doorway of my hospital room. "'Go in with a smile, come out with a smile,' that's what my Aunt Dixie used to say," she said. Five milligrams of morphine performed the work that twenty years of therapy had failed to accomplish: "Go away," I replied.

Back on the mat, Teresa had pinned her man; his glistening hands flapped like fish on the hook and then went quiet: general uproar, the upspring of solid Teresa, slower rise of defeated opponent, quickly followed by a civilized handshake. It is finished. O strapping 190-pound women of America, we who are about to die salute you!

Next up was Nick, whose opponent held him in a headlock for what felt like an hour. How much neck twisting can a boy take? I looked away. Hombre de Acero was making his way toward the exit. The relentless gym lights shone on his bald spot, or perhaps the light emanated from his head. I couldn't tell. When I looked back Nick's noggin was still on his shoulders and he was lifting one of his opponent's legs in such a way that the boy was forced to hop backwards before crashing to the ground.

The ground. The muddy ground, so different from heaven with its whizzing planets, icy comets, and cold-hearted angels. We were watching the New England

Patriots fight for a playoff spot. The TV, suicidally beautiful, was lit with the glow of fading December. Miami lined up. There was a minute to go.

"Don't worry," Nick said. "No team ever retrieves its own onside kick."

"Jesus Christ," I yelled. "Now you've jinxed them."

"No," he said, "*you* jinxed them in the third quarter when you forgot to turn the mini-helmet the way we were going."

The kick bounced up and Fred Coleman hugged the ball. He sustained an enormous hit but didn't let go.

"Double jinx," I said joyously. "It's like two minuses making a plus."

It was almost impossible to rid oneself of super-stition, much harder than to break with God, whose behavior over the centuries had been truly unfath-omable (what was He thinking?), and now, on account of 9/11, the entire nation was crossing its fingers every time it crossed the street. That was an irony, of course, that even Wayne might have appreciated. The funda-mentalists had returned us to fundamentals.

"It's mainly Christian, you know," I said to Nick.

"What is?"

The Patriots were hugging and smacking each other all over the field.

"Our superstitions: unlucky thirteen, the apostles at the Last Supper; touch wood, fingering a piece of the cross; don't walk under a ladder, the shadow thrown by Jesus bearing the cross."

"Oh, yeah." Nick twisted in his seat.

"Then there are the Jews, with their spitting and evil eyes, and the blue lintels on Arab doorways to ward off trouble. Now 'bad things come in threes' is a different story. It's trench talk: strike a match and the enemy sees, light your cigarette and he takes aim, first puff and you're smoke."

"Hey, Mom!" Nick called out. "Dad's lecturing."

At Foxborough Stadium the lights burned blue and yellow. A good number of the Patriots players pointed skyward and then clapped their hands to their hearts as a way of thanking God, who had helped them to victory while, in His picky way, choosing to send their opponents to ignominious defeat. It was axiomatic that in America, for the last two decades at least, God, like everyone else, had developed a consuming interest in the worlds of sports and entertainment and was forever helping individuals toward triumphs and rewards. He didn't seem to like losers much, and they never thanked him.

The TV went to commercial—there was a fireman's helmet and then a flag and then the name of an insurance company. The insurance company had decided to show the helmet and the flag against a background of stirring music. My wife had a claim lodged against this particular company on account of travel plans that she had canceled in order to better nurse Nick in his summer of mononucleosis eighteen months ago. She had taken out the policy to cover her fare but the company was quite sure that Nick had a "preexisting condition" and didn't feel inclined to pay up. We were appealing.

Nick clicked the remote and the screen went blank. The world was rocking off its axis. In order to help steady it, at least in the narrow confines of our TV room, I turned to the grounding subject of love.

"What happened," I asked Nick, "to that girlfriend of yours, Janis, the one with the pierced eyebrow?"

"Kissed and dismissed," he replied.

A passenger jet, its engines screaming, passed over the house on its way into Logan. I thought I might step outside and put a little lamb's blood on the lintel of the front door, but in the end I decided that, come spring, I would buy a ladder and begin to paint the house blue.

Mini-Joe

It was thirty-two years since my father died, and I had a pain like hot curry in my left shoulder. Bathylle, Dr. Da Silva's nurse, directed me into his office. She told me to take my shirt off and then she left me alone. I was there for about twenty minutes, so I started to use the doctor's phone. I dialed my wife. She wasn't home. I was about to call a couple of friends when the phone rang. "Cardiology," I answered, but whoever it was hung up. I star-sixty-nined the caller, but no one responded. I made one more call, to an old girlfriend, Alison Zawicki, whom I hadn't seen for twenty years. I'd found her number while fooling around on the Internet's "Search for a Person" and transferred it to a small piece of paper, which I'd carried around in my wallet for a month. Alison's voice, when I got through to chilly Edwardsville, Illinois, was, I thought, constricted by the smoky lassoes of time and nostalgia, but it turned out that she was eating a tangerine. Since 1976, when we had parted in anger, joy, and pouring rain outside the Hungarian Pastry Shop on New York's Amsterdam Avenue, Alison had married, raised three children, lost her mother to cancer and then her husband on account of an affair that Alison had unwisely embarked upon with a colleague in Marketing. In an impressive coincidence, her sons' middle names were the same as my sons' first names.

"How are *you*?" she asked.

I told her.

"You wait twenty years and then you call me when you've got a punch in the heart and fire rushing down your arm. That's nice."

"It's only a pain in my shoulder," I corrected, "but you're right. It's bad timing. I'm sorry to have intruded on your life. I won't phone again."

"Oh yes, you will. This has got to be at least a two-parter. Of the lousy men that I've slept with over the years, you could be the first to die. If you don't pull through, maybe someone in your family can give me a buzz."

"I'll see what I can arrange," I replied.

We talked for a while about a spring afternoon when we had cycled uptown to the Cloisters. The sky was crystal blue and the wind over the Hudson blew hard toward the Palisades. On hills our young legs hardly required the aid of gears. We kissed at a stoplight. At this point in our long-distance conversation the unicorn of blissful memory lay its head in our laps. We stroked and caressed it until it fell asleep.

"My life has been full of disappointment and regret," Alison concluded, "and I'm sorry I stood you up that night at the Ninety-second Street Y."

"That must have been someone else," I replied. "I've never been there."

Nurse Bathylle poked her head around the door. When she saw the receiver in my hand she gave me a scathing look.

"The doctor will be with you shortly."

"It rang," I said, and put the phone down on Alison.

For the next half hour I read the *PennStater,* which had been left lying on the doctor's desk. I have a soft spot for Pennsylvania, which I have never visited. I have sometimes entertained the fantasy that I am walking home past the steel mills in Bethlehem after a hard-fought high school football game. There's a light drizzle. I'm covered in mud and on my way, like the young Tom Cruise in *All the Right Moves,* to visit a Catholic girlfriend who has long red hair. When I get to her place I have a shower. She lies on the bed reading because, unlike myself, she has ambitions in the direction of college. When I come out of the shower she puts the book down and we make love.

It turned out that via the *PennStater* you could

order a life-size or mini cardboard cut-out of the university's football coach, Joe Paterno. I didn't want to do this, but I wouldn't have minded the souvenir inkstand embossed with the college crest. There were two very boring articles in the magazine, one about environmental engineering and the other focused on a local muralist. I was reading "Alumni Notes, Class of '57" when Dr. Da Silva entered the room.

"It's an odd coincidence," he said, after perusing the results of my MRI and the minutes of my various stress tests. "You were fifteen when your father died, and now you have a fifteen-year-old son."

"But I'm not dying," I insisted.

"That remains to be seen," Da Silva replied. I thought he was probably kidding.

Da Silva ran through a lot of questions of the sort everyone knows. Then he said, "I have to ask you something. The answer won't go on your medical record. Have you ever used cocaine?"

"Why?" I replied. "Do you have some?"

It was the wrong answer.

"According to your thallium stress test, your left anterior circumflex may be partially blocked," he continued after a swift elision of my ten snorts in thirty years. "You need an angiogram, then possibly angioplasty." He spilled out a few more sentences, all of which featured the words "heart disease." I didn't like this at all. By the end of forty-five minutes I had fallen down a dank well. At the bottom there was nothing interesting to eat or drink and two large containers of beta-blockers and Pravachol. As a coda to our discussion, Da Silva explained what he planned to do to me.

"The process begins," he said, "when we freeze your groin area."

"No need to bother," I replied. "I've been married for seventeen years."

"Then we rub in some of that new ointment that restores hair but makes you impotent."

Da Silva didn't so much say this as imply it. I thought of the black waves that topped off mini–Joe Paterno and complemented his Roy Orbison glasses.

"What about exercise?" I asked. I had no intention of doing any, but I was trying to ingratiate myself after the cocaine revelations. After all, this man was going to be splashing my heart with dye, then running a plumber's line down the bloody streams through which my life coursed.

"Do you own a treadmill?"

"No."

"You could try walking the mall."

I groaned.

"Thirty circuits from Bloomingdale's around the fountain to Filene's is three miles. It's free and warm. You get the camaraderie of a crowd and the entertainment of various shop windows. I recommend it to all my patients who can't afford a home gymnasium."

"See Rome and die," I said.

I didn't go to the mall, or home. Instead, I drove to O'Flanagan's bar and ordered a glass of blood-oxidizing red wine. The local paper was lying in a pool of beer farther up the counter. I fished it out and turned to Police Beat. Item 1: Local flasher seen again at the library. Item 2: Four girls from the high school spend Saturday night in the hospital emergency room having their stomachs pumped. I had already heard about 2. The girls had drunk a bottle of vodka as if it were Evian. Two slumped unconscious for three hours; the others were choking on vomit when the cops and ambulance crew arrived. I knew the mother of one of these girls. She was a hardworking person, full of love and care for her children. Her husband wasn't in the picture anymore. Every day, she made school lunches and sent her offspring on the clamorous bus to struggle with algebra, read multicultural poetry, and learn a few words of Spanish. At night she made dinner, laundered her children's clothes, helped with the homework, then drove to rent videos and Nintendo games. Sometimes she shouted, warned, and threatened, sometimes hugged.

Everybody agreed that having your stomach pumped was something to be avoided, but youth would rather swig grain alcohol and try to make death drunk than stand lost in thought with a finger to its lips.

I ordered another glass of wine.

When I got home there was a message from my cousin Daphne on my voice mail.

"I've had it confirmed," she began, "that Meyer Schloss, your grandfather on your father's side's nephew, and husband to my mother's aunt Raisl Oskerovitz, was

21

badly treated by your family on a station platform in London after the war. I'll be in and out all day."

I called her at work. There was a high-tech crackling on the line, like ice on the River Neva pulling apart in spring. My cousin was a psychotherapist. You could only reach her ten minutes out of every hour.

"Bad news for the royal line," I announced. "I'm down for an angiogram."

My cousin shrieked, but then she settled down to business.

It was 1947. The smoke from a recently arrived steam train billowed and flattened under the great roof of Victoria Station. My grandfather, the well-known pigeon fancier, religious fanatic, and specialist in unemployment, stood with his three sons in the penumbra cast by the black cylinder of the train. My father held the *News Chronicle* under his arm: headline, SIX-WAY SPY WAS SO SHY. Down the platform, clutching the refugee's obligatory brown suitcase, came skinny Meyer Schloss. Because sometimes the eye sees less than the heart knows, my family apparently missed history's misery sliding down Meyer's sloped shoulders: the camps, for example, of which they could not speak, and the DP camps that, over a period of eighteen months, had softened Meyer's jowls in a direction away from skeletal.

Well, well, after a week Gramps sent him back. No room at the inn. Too many hungry mouths to feed. No work, no beans. Bye-bye, cousin Schloss, the moil of London is not for you, nor its mohels for your children. Return to the displacement camp of your choice, and here's five quid for a new suit and a decent meal on the boat.

"I don't believe a word of it," I replied when my cousin was through. "In the first place, my grandfather never went anywhere in a collective. Second, he never had five pounds to his name, which is one of the reasons my grandmother kicked him out. And third, my father once saved a sparrow by splinting a matchstick to its broken leg. Is that the kind of man who would spurn a needy relative?"

"Hitler was a vegetarian," my cousin replied.

I lay on the hospital bed while a nurse shaved my pubic hair to centerfold specifications, then popped me a few pills to make life seem easy and calm. It was six-thirty a.m. The winter sky was the color of a wild goose's belly. Beneath it, cinder forms in high blocks ordered the patient to look no further. The real prisons, said Albert Camus, are the hospitals, and the real hospitals are the prisons. My wife and her sister sat chatting at the foot of the bed.

"What do you think?" my wife asked. "Plates or paper plates?"

"It's a party," her sister Minna replied. "You don't want to have to do a lot of cleaning up afterward."

Was it "party" she said, or "wake"? Could it be check-out time for yours truly? Or was it the drugs listening? But why not move on and out? What was there to return to in the quiet suburbs except a month of snow shoveling, the endless chauffeuring of children, and a slowly defrosting groin? On the other hand, my legacy was incomplete. On this day of potential reckoning I had offered a particularly weak and disappointing choice of last words to be remembered by.

"Can you bring up some toilet paper?"

"Yes, I'm a bit scared."

"I know which parking lot."

"Can I have a Valium drip?"

"I hate slippers."

Dr. Da Silva and his team were waiting for me in the operating theater. His assistant, Dr. Soo-Hoo, looked especially fetching in her gray scrub suit and matching mask. I wanted to ask her to dance, but my condom catheter got in fantasy's way. Lights. Camera. Action. We were in hyperspace. My upper torso burned from the inside out.

"O lac," I urged, "suspends ton vol."

These were the first words that I had uttered in French since completing the British equivalent of sixth grade. Time rested its aluminum heel on my chest but didn't stomp. Then it was over.

Dr. Da Silva leaned in and whispered close to my ear.

"May your children's arteries be as yours, yea unto the tenth generation."

Was this a blessing or a curse?

Dr. Soo-Hoo removed her mask.

"The thallium test was a false positive. It happens

only five percent of the time, and almost exclusively to women."

My wife and Minna were waiting in recovery.

"I'm clean," I announced, giving a thumbs-up sign from the supine position.

"We heard," my wife replied. "You have the heart of a girl."

I lay back. The entire futile world that I was so happy to be a part of returned to me in the shape of a white globe and its rip cord flex. My wife squeezed my hand. I thought, on reflection, that my grandfather might have been kinder to his skinny nephew Schloss. And I myself would try to do better in every way. I turned my face toward my wife's.

"Did you bring any chocolate?" I asked.

Mother
with
Child

My mother and I drive in to the Old City through Jaffa Gate and get stuck behind three donkeys and a bagel cart. Two feet away from the car a boy juices orange halves with quick up-and-down motions on a silver crusher.

"See that?" my mother says.

She's not looking at the boy but farther down the street toward a graceful Armenian arch vaulting across the sky into the side of a church.

"Reminds me of that horrible railway bridge on Park Avenue," she says. "Dark, dirty, disgusting place."

"This is not the old neighborhood," I tell her. "This is not northwest London."

"I don't care where we are."

"Then what exactly is the problem?"

After a few fake sniffles she manages to get out, "They might have said I looked pretty."

We have just come from visiting Rachel and Aron Belz—her first cousins, her only relatives in Israel, and practically her only living relatives on the globe. She had never met them before. As we left the house, where I have been eating Friday night dinners throughout my nine-month sabbatical here, she loud-whispered, "Horrible accents. Poles." And they heard. These poor bastards who spent half of the Second World War hiding in a forest and the other half starving in the camps. These decent, hospitable people for whom acknowledging my mother's looks did not top the list of "Things to do if we survive, even if we don't get the chance for fifty years."

"You're seventy-four. It's not the kind of compliment that always springs to mind."

"Well, that I had a pretty dress, then."

She goes back to tears.

The donkey in front of us looses a broad stream onto the road. I look across at my mother and have an ugly association, one of the worst she's ever inspired in me. It's 1979, and I'm driving home from university. Some old drunk totters across the road, gets caught in my lights, and freezes. When he moves again it's to raise his thumb into hitchhiking position. I open the door and he falls into the car. Almost as soon as he sits down there's a terrible smell.

"I'm sorry," he says. "I've shat meself."

We drive eighteen miles to Clacton-on-Sea, then he gets out. The seat has a little stain and a thin brown liquid sheen.

My mother's moved on to another topic. Her favorite.

"You come here, to a land of Jews, and you find the only *yok* in Jerusalem."

"She came with me. We met in London. You know that."

"She's still a *yok*."

Yok is Anglo-Jewish for "gentile." It's worse than *goy* or *shiksa*. It connotes viciousness, brutality, and deep, irredeemable stupidity. And my mother hasn't even met her.

"What's more, she's got 'Christ' in her name."

"Her name's Tina."

"What do you think that's short for, genius?"

Right then I decide two things: not to tell my mother that Tina and I are on the verge of breaking up (why should I make her happy?), and to return my mother, as speedily as possible, to her hotel.

I reverse the car, and then circle around the back of the Old City. Halfway down the Mount of Olives, the burnished onion domes of the Russian Orthodox Church, patched with snow, gleam in the February sunlight. It's my turn to say "See that?"

My mother, the blinkered horse, refuses to turn her head.

"It's your life," she says.

"That's right."

"Drop me off here!" she suddenly screams. "I can't bear to be with you anymore."

"Here" happens to be the Arab bus station outside the Damascus Gate, where we are stuck at the light. People jostle for space, spill out of unruly lines, slip through brown belches of exhaust fumes. Then a demonstration comes around the corner—a couple hundred men who aren't pleased with Arafat and are less pleased with the Israeli government.

"Oh, shit," I say.

My mother makes as if to open the car door.

"Go on," I say. "What's keeping you?"

A woman with a basket of plums on her head dips to offer us her merchandise. The bruised, split ripeness of the fruit, the whole sensual/sexual/violent fiasco of the place—plums *and* snow *and* yelling fundamentalists— is too much for my mother (it's too much for everyone).

"No *thank* you," she says, in her best regal-imitation phone voice.

I think of setting her on a bus bound for one of the newly autonomous areas on the West Bank, maybe Jericho—someplace where the old are respected simply for being old and personality is overlooked.

At the King Solomon Hotel I pull up adjacent to the shaded entranceway. She gets out and slams the car door. Immediately, an elderly gentleman in a white suit, who, according to my mother, has been stalking her with intent to rape, steps out of the shadows; he's like an overweight Jay Gatsby.

"Mrs. Samuels. You're back! And this must be your son."

"He used to be my son."

Fat Gatsby looks baffled for a moment. But no, my mother's response is a familiar one after all.

"All children disappoint their parents," he says, but I can tell from his sweet, tanned, chubby face that he doesn't believe this; he's simply trying to ingratiate himself with my mother.

My mother gives me "the stare": she tries to do something with her eyes that will communicate hurt, annoyance, pathos, bathos, loneliness, and unyielding, mulish obstinacy. It's a brave but doomed piece of acting.

I drive off. In the rearview mirror I see Gatsby waving. My mother has disappeared in the spin of the revolving doors.

In the parking lot behind my apartment block on King George Street, the snow from the previous night has melted. I have to splash through a couple of icy puddles on my way in. As I push open the door to the building, Tina steps out from behind a large blue van. She looks about half an hour into her Ophelia impression: Millais hair, eyes wild, face drained of blood.

"You can't leave me."

I turn around like a coward and start to run back through the lot.

She pursues me, yelling, "What about the children?"

This stops me in my tracks.

"We don't *have* any children."

"But we could."

"Not if you keep sleeping with other people."

"It was one night."

"It was *many* nights."

She weighs this in her mind, like Yasmin, the woman who sells vegetables door to door and comes with a scale and three rocks, balancing what she wants against what she thinks she can get.

"At the time you didn't seem to care," she says.

"What gave you that impression?"

"You didn't stop sleeping with me, did you?"

"That's different."

I have no idea what it is different from. In fact, I feel exposed. She's right; there have been times in our relationship when appetite overcame jealousy.

"How's your mother? When am I going to meet her?"

I start to labor up the hill.

"I want to go to the desert!" Tina shouts after me.

The last time that we were in the Sinai she threatened to drown herself in the Red Sea. She got drunk on cheap brandy, sang the biological clock verse from Bonnie Raitt's "Nick of Time," then ran fully clothed into the waves. I watched her head bob in the moonlight, and then it disappeared and the next time I saw her she was lying facedown on the dark apron of sand about a hundred yards upshore from where she'd set out. I approached at a run—stoned, out of breath, the stars wheeling around like crazed gulls. I said, "Are you all right?" and she replied, "You didn't try to save me."

It was true. On the other hand, as she well knows, because it is a source of great embarrassment to me, I can't swim. My mother, bless her heart, sent me to elocution lessons when all the other kids headed off to the pool.

I jog all the way down Shatz Street and up King George until I get to Independence Park. I buy a newspaper at a small kiosk from a man I've never seen before, who gives me a look of burning hatred, and take the paper into the Rondo Café.

While I'm drinking their lukewarm coffee I have one of those ideas that in retrospect seem so bizarre that they can be explained only by the action of chemical forces in the brain over which the individual has no control. *She wants to meet my mother,* I think. *Then let's all go to the desert.*

The following day, we pick my mother up at her hotel at seven a.m. She's wearing something in patriotic blue and white that she calls a "trouser suit"—her clothes are much too hot for the desert, even in February, but we'll deal with that later. Tina, for her part, has decided to play it straight. She's got her hair pulled back and is wearing jeans and one of those embroidered peasant shirts that can be viewed as either conservative or hip, depending on your politics.

My mother insists on sitting in the front seat because of her legs, which, though shorter than everybody else's, are apparently too long for the back seat.

"Hello, dear," she says to Tina, her religious prejudices falling away miraculously in the presence of someone who might possibly be charmed.

"Hello, Mrs. Samuels. Nice to meet you, finally."

"Oh, do call me Barbara," says my mother.

"I'd love to," Tina replies.

"William's going to take us for a nice ride."

Tina gives a tight little smile. "Have you ever been to the Sinai, Barbara?"

"The Sinai?" replies my mother, pronouncing the first syllable "sin" instead of "sign," in an attempt to sound classy. "I don't think I have."

"Don't think"! This is a person who up until one week ago chose not to go *anywhere* other than the streets of northwest London and a couple of deathly South Coast resorts with "Jewish" hotels.

"It's beautiful," Tina says.

My mother responds as if Tina had said "*You're* beautiful," and after a moment I realize it is because those are the words that she has chosen to hear.

"Thank you, dear. I was always a pretty girl, and as you see"—face tap—"no wrinkles."

"And how old are you, Barbara?"

"She's seventy-four," I say. "She was forty-one when I was born. You see, there's no need to rush."

Why am I doing this?

We take the new road down to the Dead Sea so that no one will throw rocks at us. My mother tends to regard Palestinians in the same way that she treated the Russian Orthodox Church on the Mount of Olives:

33

theoretically she's willing to acknowledge their existence, but she would really prefer not to look. Tina, on the other hand, believes herself to be a great internationalist and a friend to all. Like most Brits, she is a powerful defender of the insulted and the injured, except if they happen to be Irish. During our year here, she has attended every Peace Now rally. In fact, it was at one of these gatherings that she met Joel Lemkowitz, ace foreign correspondent of the *New York Something or Other,* a man with impressive credentials, and a believer, apparently, in frequent, unprotected sex with other men's girlfriends. ("I'm thirty-five—I *want* to have a baby.")

The fan on the passenger side of the dashboard whirrs. My mother clutches at her hair as if her whole fluffed-out gray do might fly off.

"Switch it off! Switch it off! What are you doing, you idiot?"

"Trying to cool you down."

"I'm perfectly cool."

She stares straight ahead at the unwinding ribbon of road. Her knees are pressed tightly together, and her white handbag rests primly on top of them.

In the car mirror I see Tina slowly lift her peasant shirt to show me that she isn't wearing a bra.

At Ein Bokek, we park and head for the beach café next door to the psoriasis center that sits on the shores of the Dead Sea. Two tall pale men in white sarongs, their scaly skin exposed, walk past our table and head toward the soothing mud pile at the edge of the water.

"Who are they?" asks my mother.

"How should I know?" I say. "A Danish actuary and his orthodontist friend."

"Whoever they are, they shouldn't be allowed to walk around like that."

"Why not? Are the Nuremberg laws in effect here?"

"Don't joke about the Holy Cost."

It is a brilliant stroke of my mother's to turn "Holocaust" into a kind of Irish pronunciation of "Holy Ghost." Oddly enough, for all her supposed deep-seated Jewish feeling, there's nothing she likes better than being told she doesn't look Jewish.

"I was in Germany once," Tina puts in. "On my way back from Denmark. I had a boyfriend in Copenhagen. A wonderful poet. I met him at the student hostel. He took me to Tivoli Gardens. His name was Niels Nordbrandt."

"*Den*mark," says my mother, her voice a low, throbbing imitation of something seductive. "How very interesting."

Tina goes back to the car to change into her swimsuit. To my astonishment my mother decides to take to the water too. I locate the changing room for her. She disappears inside, then emerges ten minutes later looking very "pretty," by which I mean she's advancing down the concrete path in one-piece and heels as if it were a catwalk. We get to the edge of the water and, while I'm trying to get my mother afloat, which is like pushing a rowboat out to sea, I hear Tina, who is already immersed, yell cheerfully, "I've got salt up my cunt!"

She waves gaily while a flotilla of German and Scandinavian tourists wildly start to paddle their salt-slicked bodies in her direction as if she's announced that the bar is open for business. Most floaters clasp their knees and tool around in racing-driver position, but my mother has unfortunately turned on her front and, legs and arms up in Flying Nun mode, appears to be heading quite fast, O blessed current, in the direction of Jordan.

"Come on in," Tina yells. "You can't drown."

I wave back and point to my shoes, an obscure gesture that I hope she will interpret in some way favorable to me.

After they have showered and changed and had something to drink, my mother says she's tired and would like to return to her hotel. She'll save the Sinai for another time.

Almost as soon as we start to drive, my mother falls asleep, or perhaps she has quietly died in the front seat. Tina starts doing the shirt thing again.

"Pull over and come in the back," she says.

"Don't be ridiculous. We're not sixteen."

"She won't wake up."

"Tina, please."

"It's all that sun and sand."

"And salt."

"I'm ovulating. I took my temperature with the basal thermometer before we set out."

I drive as if I haven't heard. I decide that I am drawn to desperation, the way some men are attracted to large

36

breasts, because I am the son of a woman who pretends never to need anything.

Cold air hits us as soon as we start to climb; by the time we get back to Jerusalem, Tina's shivering and the chill has woken my mother up. In the driveway of the King Solomon, an ambulance pulls sharply in front of us. We get out of the car and see Fat Gatsby being wheeled by on a stretcher. He's got an oxygen mask over his nose and mouth but manages to wave feebly at my mother, who ignores him completely. (At the funeral of her best friend's husband she asked me, "Why is the rabbi talking about Alfie so much? He's dead.")

"Bye, Barbara," Tina says.

"Yes," my mother replies, expressing a hope.

Back at our apartment, we go into the bedroom. Tina takes off all her clothes, then starts to unbutton and unzip mine.

"Do your duty," she says when we're both naked. "You've oppressed women for thousands of years."

I reach for her. She takes half a step back.

"Now, about those babies?"

She moves forward again, presses her upper torso onto mine, delivers her hand into my groin, and repeats the question.

In this kind of situation, the options are strictly limited, so I say something vaguely encouraging. But the moment I speak, the room's warm air is filled with clanging bells, alarms, sighs, the call of the muezzin, rabbinical wailing, the roar of a protesting crowd, the righteous shrieks of my critics, who can't fail to note my Jewish self-hatred, my ego-driven refusal to accommodate simple desires, my jokes at the expense of the opposite sex, and—rightly, it seems, as we fall on the bed—it doesn't matter what I say.

Dead
Ringers

Henry, lying on a table in the ultrasound room, felt the young nurse spread warm jelly over his testicles. He tried to fight back an erection and, somewhat disappointingly, succeeded with ease.

"See anything so far?"

The nurse click-clacked on the machine and slid a probe over him. The screen flashed black and white; there were constellations of electronic blips, universes, black holes.

"The doctor will talk to you afterward."

The nurse was on automatic pilot. What possible interest could middle-aged balls hold for her?

"Turn on your side, please. No, the other side."

Henry turned, and the pain throbbed through him. He was there because of the pain. And the pain was there because . . . well, because pain comes and takes you by surprise. Sometimes, as in his case, it persists.

He had spoken first with Dr. Vikrami. She was his wife's doctor first, but because he was too lazy to search for someone else Henry had signed on too. In most matters Dr. Vikrami was straightforward, to the point, almost brusque, but she seemed to regard Henry's private parts as just that. Once a year she lifted the band of his underpants, took a quick look, then snapped the elastic back without comment, as if what she had seen had somehow offended her. Last March, as Henry was getting dressed, she had muttered, "And how is your sex life? Everything all right?" Henry had begun to reply but as soon as he did so Dr. Vikrami left the room.

Back home, he complained to Arlene.

"But what do you want her to do?" his wife responded in an exasperated voice.

"I want her to examine me thoroughly."

"You should go to a male doctor."

"That's ridiculous. All doctors should provide the same treatment. They're doctors; it's like being a neutral country."

When Henry called Dr. Vikrami and described the pain in his testicles, she did not ask him to come in.

"See?" Henry put his hand over the receiver and hissed at Arlene, who was working in the kitchen.

"I think we had better set you up with the radiologist right away."

"Do you think it's serious?"

"Let me make a phone call and I'll get right back to you."

She was as good as her word.

"Tomorrow. Eight-fifteen. At the hospital. Can you make that?"

Henry couldn't sleep. He channel-surfed for an hour and thumped his pillows. Arlene woke up.

"I'm going to die," Henry said.

"So's everyone else," Arlene murmured, and turned her back to him.

The pain, like so much that had affected Henry's life in a big way, was connected to sex. For some time Arlene had been complaining of sore breasts; she didn't want to be touched. She and Henry had fought terribly, sadly, after her father had died six months previously. She had accused him of being insensitive, indifferent to her suffering, unable to take care of the children properly. He continued to be sexually demanding, he hadn't allowed her time to herself, time to mourn. Henry thought the accusations unjustified. He had liked his father-in-law and he missed him too.

The sore breasts had arrived within two weeks of the funeral. But last week, after watching a repeat episode of *The Jewel in the Crown* on PBS, Arlene had suddenly relented and let him push her nightdress up. At the sight of those gorgeous orbs Henry ejaculated, and with the hot spurt came searing pain. He lay facedown on his pillow.

"Too much for you?" Arlene asked, tucking herself back into a cocoon and rolling onto her side.

He didn't want to mention the pain; it seemed like a defeat.

The radiologist came into the room. She was even more attractive than the nurse. A lion's mane of tawny hair, freckles on her snub nose. Henry lay there in his hospital johnny, trying to tug the bottom down like the hem of a skirt.

"Mr. Newman?"

Henry nodded.

"How are you feeling?"

He thought, *Tell me the worst.*

"Well, I'm happy to say we can't find much wrong with you. Your epididymis is inflamed, but not remarkably so."

"What's the epididymis?"

"It's the mass at the back of your testes. You've got some convoluted tubes back *here*"—she prodded under his skirt with her fingers—"and they've gotten inflamed. It's not uncommon in men of your age."

"Is it curable?"

"Possibly, or it may be that you have developed a chronic condition. In which case, I'm afraid, it's just something that you're going to have to live with. Are you under stress?"

"All the time."

The radiologist laughed, a sweet, melodic laugh. Henry wanted to say "Marry me."

"You should probably consult a urologist. Just to get some advice. I'll give you a name before you leave."

The route home took him past the Star of David Convalescent Home on VFW Parkway. Without realizing that he had made a decision to do so, he pulled into the parking lot. An old man with an aluminum walker inched away from the car next to him. Henry tried to stop himself from springing out so as not to emphasize the terrible difference between middle and old age.

His mother was sitting up in bed, eating a green apple. Her roommate, Mrs. Sonnenthal, bolt upright in a chair, held a magazine in her lap but didn't look as if she had been reading it. From her window his mother could see the fake gingerbread roof of a Pancake House. Two weeks ago someone had been shot dead in the parking lot. The police suspected a drug deal gone bad.

"What, no boyfriends today?" Henry asked teasingly.

"Your son has a virile imagination," Mrs. Sonnenthal replied, not smiling.

"How are you doing, Mom?" Henry tried to keep up the lighthearted tone.

"I'm on my way out."

"Mom, you're not even dressed."

"Not outside, lummox. Out of this earth. Death."

"Your mother's very tired," Mrs. Sonnenthal added. "She's had a visitor."

"Who?"

"Mr. Flu."

"Why didn't you tell me?"

His mother shrugged her fragile shoulders.

"One week we could be here," Mrs. Sonnenthal continued, "the next you'll find an empty room."

Henry felt his heart empty out like a burst dam.

"But the doctor. I had a word with him on the way in. He said you were doing fine."

"Since when have they known anything?"

Henry wanted to say "They know the difference between epididymitis and testicular cancer."

His mother pulled her bed jacket tighter around her and shivered. The skin at her neck hung loose and red.

"Never mind all this," she said. "Have you been *there*?"

There was the heart of the matter. She repeated the question on his every visit. Three months ago, shortly after her eightieth birthday, his mother had suddenly become concerned about Henry's brother's grave. Henry had lived forty-seven years without it ever being mentioned, but now here it was, in the foreground of things.

His brother had died as a baby two years before Henry was born. He lived seven months, then he caught an infection and died. It was shortly after Pearl Harbor. His father had been mobilized and his mother left alone. When Henry was growing up the baby was rarely mentioned. No one visited his grave. No memorial candle was lit. Henry couldn't remember learning the name until he was about ten: Aubrey.

His mother and Mrs. Sonnenthal were looking expectantly at him, waiting for a reply.

"No, Ma, I haven't been yet. I've been busy. I've got things to do."

The two women sighed, simultaneously it seemed, old, exhausted sighs that appeared to test their lung capacity and rattle something inside them.

"I'll go. I promise."

"You'll go." Mrs. Sonnenthal was scathing.

He wanted to say "This has nothing to do with *you*," but he was afraid to offend her. She was his mother's only friend, only confidante. What if she abandoned her, or requested a room change?

His mother picked up a comb from her bedside table and pulled it through her thin gray locks.

"Pass me that mirror," she ordered him. Henry did so, and she seemed to relent.

"And how are you? You all right? You look a bit fat."

"I'm OK. I'm swimming." The throbbing in his epididymis caused Henry to shift in his seat.

"The children?"

"Fine."

"Arlene?"

She didn't wait to hear his reply.

"Why aren't you at work?"

"I'm on my way. I thought I'd stop . . ."

"You're coming from a strange direction at this time of the morning. Where have you been?"

"Nowhere. I just thought I'd drop in."

A young girl in blue overalls came smartly through

the door, pushing a trolley laden with brooms and pans.

"Time to get up," she announced in a thick Irish brogue. "I've got to clean this room out."

"Come back in five minutes," Mrs. Sonnenthal ordered her. "This one's visiting his mother."

When the girl left the room Mrs. Sonnenthal whispered, "She's illegal. They all are. She's got no Social Security. What if she gets sick, that's what I want to know."

Henry left down a corridor choked with slow-moving individuals in bathrobes, some with sticks, some on metal walkers, all bent or stooped, making the effort.

He decided to take the morning off. He called Angela at the office. Things were slow anyway. No one had any money, not for the kind of investments he specialized in: low-cost housing programs for corporations who wanted to get a tax break and look good at the same time.

He went early to the swimming pool at his health club. Swimming brought temporary relief from the pain—something to do with gravity.

In the large room next to the pool, women in brightly colored spandex stepped up and down on tiny stairways. He watched through the big picture windows until all the women suddenly turned at once. He held up his hands in a futile gesture of surrender and walked on through a double set of padded swinging doors.

Dead Ringers

Swimming was boring. Worse, the club insisted that you wear a cap, which he hated. Henry's was black, with a sharp red logo on the side connoting muscularity and athleticism, but even so. This morning, in order to entertain himself, he tried to recall what it had been like to be the age of his lap number. One through four were entirely lost to him, but on five he remembered the first day of school, and by ten his memory banks had begun to release some funds. On lap eighteen—late for a boy, he knew—came sex. Henry was breathing hard now, and he took in a mouthful of water halfway down the lane. When Carol Anne Lourdes appeared before him on the beige couch in the basement of her parents' house he was embarrassed to feel the erection that had eluded him at the radiologist's begin an underwater rise. In the next lane a man with a shaved head (no cap required) and a sumo stomach heaved himself out of the water to be replaced by a man with a withered arm who dragged himself up the pool in slow sidestrokes.

When Henry was done he went and sat in the whirlpool. Two women, submerged up to their necks in bubbling water, were discussing surgeries (it was the endless topic). Henry closed his eyes and felt white water beat against his back.

"Excuse me," one of the women shouted across at him. "Can you help us out? What do you call the operation that men have in the groin area that begins with a *p*?"

"Prostate," Henry yelled back confidently.

"Is it in the penis or in the balls?"

Henry realized that he didn't know. He was pretty sure it wasn't in the penis, but he didn't think it was in the balls either. But then, where could it be? And why hadn't the woman said "testicles"? "Penis" and "balls" didn't go.

He pretended that he hadn't heard and sank deeper into the tub.

When he had showered and dressed he called Arlene from a booth outside the cafeteria.

"What did the doctor say?"

"There's nothing wrong."

"Well, that's good."

"Not exactly nothing. Epididymitis."

"Oh, that's just an inflammation."

Henry had seen a sign once stapled to a telephone pole near his house. It said, FOR SALE, FULL SET OF EN-CYCLOPEDIA BRITANNICA, PERFECT CONDITION, UNUSED, WIFE KNOWS FUCKING EVERYTHING.

"Are you at the office?"

"Yes."

"What time are you coming home?"

"I don't know. Later. I've got a lot on."

Henry put the phone down. He didn't know quite why he had lied. He had nothing to hide.

He got in his car and drove aimlessly, or so he thought, but as the neighborhoods changed and the houses became noticeably less affluent he knew that he was headed toward the cemetery where his brother was buried.

He listened to the DJ on the radio announce "WJXP Boston, no rap and *nooooo* hard rock." Every time he heard these words Henry felt crushed. He wanted desperately to be with the rap and rock listeners, to eschew the endless loop of James Taylor and Fleetwood Mac. It was a problem for people in his generation. Even those with teenage children couldn't get it into their heads that they weren't young anymore, so the radio stations had taken it upon themselves to remind them.

Henry stood in the cemetery office on one side of a high desk. A short woman detached herself from conversation with a man in a black silk yarmulke and came to talk to him. Henry explained the situation. She reached under the desk and extracted a battered ledger with the legend 1942 embossed in gold on the front.

"Newman, you say."

"Or it could be Neuman. My father changed his name, but I'm not sure exactly when. It was before I was born."

"And this is your brother you're looking for?"

"Yes."

"Sad for you."

Was it? Henry wasn't sure. Sad for his parents, certainly. But what was Aubrey to him? A chimera, a

49

figment of the imagination, and not a very powerful one at that.

"Was it January 1942?"

"January or February. Sometime in winter. My father was away. They gave him leave to come back."

The woman pored over the handwritten pages.

"Here we are. Aubrey Neuman. Two-sixteen, 1942. FF seventy-three. That's in the old cemetery. You'll have to walk across the street. Mr. Gesell will direct you."

Henry walked past rows of graves, some freshly dug, some with fresh-cut flowers in small glass vases, others with small pebbles placed as tokens of memory. In the lower half where his brother lay, the tombstones were smaller and the chisel work less elegant. The community had been poorer then.

In a far corner where the paved paths gave way to gravel walkways, Henry found the marker FF. It had begun to rain, a warm drizzle that misted and sparkled the stones. Heading down the line 51–100, Henry tripped and stumbled to the ground. When he stood and brushed himself off he noticed that his hand was bleeding from a small cut. He found a tissue in his pocket and pressed it to the wound.

FF73 was overgrown with weeds, and the tiny tombstone, chipped and streaked with bird shit, had tilted to one side. Taking care not to step on the grave, Henry tugged with one hand at the high sprouting tendrils that clutched at the stone and obscured its inscription. At the top were some words in Hebrew that Henry couldn't understand and below them his brother's name and the dates of his short life. His parents had left a simple message of bereavement: DEEPLY MOURNED BY followed by their names.

Henry stood for a few minutes, letting the rain dampen his head. He tried to concentrate his attention on the grave, to feel something about his brother's death, but all that took his attention was the throbbing in his left testicle. The sound of footsteps diverted him and he looked up to see Gesell, the man from the office, approaching at a zigzag through a line of graves. He had swapped his yarmulke for a green felt hat.

"I followed you down," he shouted from a couple rows away. "I thought you might need a prayer."

"A prayer?"

"I can say a prayer for you. For the departed."

Henry didn't respond.

"A donation is required. At your discretion, but ten dollars is the usual amount."

"I don't think so," Henry replied, and began to walk back down the path. The rain picked up in earnest and came down in heavy, fat drops. Gesell pulled down the brim of his hat.

"I'll say something anyway."

Henry continued to walk away.

He decided to go home for lunch. When he walked in the door Arlene was on the phone. She acknowledged him with a glance and carried on talking. In recent years he had noticed she spent more and more time on the phone to her friends. Women, he felt, grew closer together as they got older, whereas men drifted further apart. Arlene was part of a tight group, an empathetic circle in which each member helped the other through crises: childrens' sicknesses and broken limbs, problems at work, divorce, the loss of their parents. Henry barely even spoke to the neighbors anymore. His best friends, or the people he liked to imagine were his best friends, lived miles away, in California, or upstate New York.

He went to the fridge, removed a chunk of cheddar, and began to make himself a sandwich. Arlene, watching him, pointed toward his heart and mouthed the word *cheese*.

Eventually, she put the phone down.

"What are you doing here?"

"I went to check out my brother's grave."

"Obedient boy. How did it go?"

He knew he had to be very careful—hence the nonchalance of that "check out"—any indication that he had been moved and Arlene would have pounced, accusing him of trying to play the sympathy card, accruing emotional capital that didn't belong to him. But in truth the grave had not touched him, so why not say so? Because after the business about her father he did not want her to think he was hard-hearted.

"It needs some work. I'll go out there with a scrubbing brush and rake. Clean it all up. Then I'll take Mom and Mrs. Sonnenthal."

"I have to get back to work."

Arlene taught speech pathology in a local school.

When she had gone Henry dialed the urologist's

number. The secretary told him that she had a cancellation and he could come in right away. Henry thought that he'd had enough of doctors for one day, but then he changed his mind. Why not get it all over with?

The urologist's office was on the top floor of a new medical building only a mile or two from Henry's suburban home. The chairs in the waiting room were tubular chrome and leather; there were two glass tables covered with upscale magazines that had single-initial titles.

"I'm here for Dr. Balter."

"Dr. Malcolm Balter or Dr. Stuart Balter?"

"I'm not sure." Henry handed over the piece of paper that the radiologist had given him.

"Dr. *Stuart* Balter—he'll be right with you. You can go through into the examining room."

When the doctor entered, tall, angular, with gold-rimmed glasses, Henry thought that he recognized him.

"Does your son play Little League?" he asked.

"You may be thinking of my nephew. I have a daughter."

"But you watch him, right? I've seen you at the games."

"That's my brother Malcolm. We're identical twins."

"You're kidding."

Dr. Balter smiled. He had had this conversation before.

"Dead Ringers!" Henry announced excitedly.

"Excuse me?"

53

"The movie. Surely people must have mentioned it to you. With Jeremy Irons. Only they're not urologists, they're . . ."

"Gynecologists."

"Yes."

There was a pause while Dr. Balter reviewed the chart that Henry had filled out.

"And you've had this problem how long?"

"About three months."

"Well, shall we take a look?"

Dr. Balter took a look, then rested Henry's left testicle gently in the palm of his hand, like a bird's egg.

"I'm going to press in various places and you tell me if it hurts."

Balter pushed with his finger.

"No. No. No. No."

"Not at all?"

"No, nothing." Henry felt like a fraud. After the fourth "no" he was hoping for pain. A shooting, serious pain, something to justify his visit to a "specialist."

"OK, turn on your side, please. Now we come to the part that nobody likes."

At this moment Henry always thought the same thing: But what if you did like it? Did that mean you were gay? The truth was that he had never not liked it; he had only worried that he would be unable to control his bladder.

Henry pulled up his pants and tucked in his shirt.

"Your prostate is fine."

Henry took a deep breath. He knew how Balter had gotten there, but where was the prostate located? Henry was too embarrassed to ask.

"Now, let me show you something."

Dr. Balter sat down in a chair next to Henry. He held up an anatomical drawing and used his finger as a pointer.

"Here's the area of your problem."

Henry looked at the swirling contours of blood and muscle. For all it meant to him he might just as well have been studying a relief map of the Mekong Delta.

Balter more or less repeated what the cute radiologist had already told him, then asked abruptly, "Any questions?"

"How do you get on with your brother?"

Balter was taken aback, and Henry too, by his own question. Nevertheless, he proceeded.

"I mean, are you close? As twins? You must feel responsible for each other."

And suddenly Henry knew what he was asking, and he wanted to shout, "His grave. Would you maintain his grave if he died?" But instead he murmured "I'm sorry" and fled the room.

The following evening after work he returned to the cemetery. He knelt by the tilting tombstone in the late-summer light and scrubbed at the stone. There was dirt in the crevices of his brother's name, which he used a toothbrush to get at. As soon as he began to exert himself his testicle throbbed, and after a while he had to pause to let the pain subside.

An hour passed; the sky streaked a kind of industrial orange that he associated with the toxic glow that rose over power plants on hot and humid days. Henry, who had forgotten to bring gloves, tore at the bushes that surrounded and overgrew the grave. He pulled some up by their roots and cast them aside; earth slid into his shoes and beneath the cuffs of his rolled-up shirtsleeves. Henry smoothed the ground and scoured the stone. By the time he was through, his face was running with sweat and smeared with mud. He felt surprisingly pleased with himself and thought that, yes, now he might cry. It wasn't tears that came next but words.

"OK now?" he asked the stone.

He washed in the bathroom nearest the entrance of the Star of David Home, then took the elevator up to his mother's floor. It was late, and she wouldn't be expecting him. The light in the corridor was the sickly fluorescent yellow that substituted for dusk in hospitals and old people's homes.

The door to the room was closed. He knocked, then gently pushed it open. Mrs. Sonnenthal was sitting in her chair; she held her purse in her lap and her legs were pressed tightly together. The room was illuminated only by the tiny blue emergency lights above the bed. She turned her eyes toward Henry.

"Your mother's gone," she said quietly.

"When will she be back?"

"Back? Back is for Christians."

Henry stared at his mother's empty bed. The white sheets were folded down and the pillow had been removed.

A shiver ran down his spine. One of the orange call lights above the bed began to blink.

"But I did it," he murmured to Mrs. Sonnenthal. "I went there."

Mrs. Sonnenthal remained immobile, an ugly grimace of contempt frozen on her face.

Henry, dazed, turned back into the corridor. The oblong light seemed to pass right through him, like an x-ray. He leaned against a wall and breathed deeply.

Then he saw his mother shuffling in slippered feet out of a bathroom. She approached him slowly, not recognizing or acknowledging his presence until she was right in front of him.

"I couldn't stand her anymore," she said. "I asked for a move."

She toppled a little to one side; Henry gripped her under the elbow.

"I cleaned up Aubrey's grave," he said.

"Thinks she's someone special because her son's an optometrist."

Henry maneuvered his mother in the direction of the water fountain. He needed a drink. "I always remember you, you know," his mother said, "even when I forget you. There's nothing wrong with you."

An
Ambulance
Is
on
the
Way

It was Tuesday. In the hanging gardens the mowers and blowers were going full blast in outboard counterpoint to the hard knocks of construction. By the aqueduct an electric cable fizzed and popped. A fireman stood close by to make sure that no one fried. There were two burglar alarms testing the wind in empty houses. Then the rain came at a heavy slant, hard and alien, like a cold sheet blown over eastern Massachusetts from the Urals.

I was one of the daytime staff of a Boston suburb, along with gardeners, illegal immigrant cleaners, builders and painters, au pairs, the mail- and garbagemen, young mothers, wives who didn't work, and academics on sabbatical. It was my job to sit in a room, stare out its window, inspect invisible currents of air, and make sure that the hungry birds were at their feeders. I was also a hunter/gatherer. I hunted around for lost keys and wallets; when I found them I went out and hunted for food in the broad overlit boulevards of local supermarkets, and then I gathered people into conversation.

What was there for tweeners in our neighborhood to talk about on a late-summer day in the orange dusk of the millennium? Children on the way up, parents on the way out were a given: movies, vacations taken and planned, and the local man, Richard Press, who, while holidaying with his family, grabbed his saxophone and played "Hail to the Chief" when Bill Clinton's sailboat, rigged with the black ear cords of Secret Service agents, docked in Menemsha. But on this particular afternoon, conversation was more sternly focused on the activities of the DiBiassio family, who with the proceeds from twenty summers of mowing and a whopping $23,000 scratch card windfall had begun construction of a garish palace in white brick on the corner of Berry Street to augment their drab colonial.

At the near end of the DiBiassios' driveway, home to the family's gardening trucks, parked in happy violation of our careful city's every zoning law, stood an alabaster pyramid. This gleaming store had been placed at the disposal of master masons employed in raising a late-twentieth-century Italianate monument to the benefits of hard work and persistent small-scale gambling.

The neighborhood was appalled: in the awkward world of "additions," nothing so blanched and extreme had ever been presented.

It was hoped by the small crowd in the Stop & Shop parking lot that I might have some altering influence on the DiBiassios' Moby Dick–like aesthetic, owing to the fact that I once played alongside Carlo DiBiassio in the back four of an over-forties soccer team. But I had nothing against quirky design, and what is more, I had always admired the palazzos of Venice, where six hundred years ago white marble graced the balustrades and bathtubs of the lucky rich. OK, so they weren't brick.

In order to prove that I could be a true friend to those who sought to stun and blind the bourgeoisie, I drove home down Berry Street. Carlo, back from a long day uprooting bushes in the deep territory of someone's two-acre yard, was sitting on the stoop with his girlfriend, Tiego, who is from Cape Verde. I stopped the car. Five years ago, on a soggy field in a torrential downpour, I had urged Carlo in the direction of matrimony. At the time Tiego was standing under a yellow umbrella, windswept and drenched, the only spectator of our ridiculous exertions.

"She comes to every game," I'd said. "Why don't you marry her?"

"You come to every game," Carlo had replied, his broad nose losing raindrops like a leaking faucet. "Should I marry you?"

Now they were sitting as if at a ball game, shelling peanuts and dropping the dry husks into the cradle of Tiego's loose cotton skirt.

"Hey, Heartbeat," Carlo said when he saw me, "how you blowing?" Then he rose and did a fair imitation of a middle-aged man staggering breathless in pursuit of a leather ball.

Tiego stood and scattered the shells. She was famous for her warm smile and appealing personality. She was also the assistant manager at a local branch of Bank-Boston and had overseen my blind dive into a second mortgage. The last time I saw her, however, I had been lying in a hospital bed, working the pathos of recuperation from a broken ankle. Tiego had come to visit me in the late afternoon of a muggy June day. She placed a vase of white freesias on the bedside table, then sat in the gray visitors' chair and related an episode involving herself, her sister-in-law, and breast size. It was the kind of story that women tell only when men are sick or incapacitated; otherwise the tomcat gets all stirred up. Here was what happened: Tiego had been walking down Sandyhook Beach earlier that day with her brother's wife, Janice, who weighs 220 pounds and has enormous breasts. Janice suddenly pulled at the top of Tiego's dress and said, "Where are your tits? You haven't even got a mouthful there." I didn't know what to say, but fortunately at that moment a nurse arrived to check my leg's elevation, and shortly after that the happy scene was rounded with a sleep.

"Tell your friends not to worry," Carlo said, anticipating the meaning of my visit and waving at the bricks. "It's not what they think. We've started but we'll never finish. I'll tell you what's going on, but don't pass the information on. As long as you're 'in construction' on a home improvement, you get a tax break.

My former neighbor in Swampscott had bricks in his yard for nineteen years. Two or three bricks a year and a slap of mortar when the inspector comes around—that's all you need."

The rain gave up and the evening settled down on a warm breeze. We were drinking grappa and talking about football, the round kind, and how life was when the three of us were young and not American. Tiego leaned forward and I looked down her dress: the mouthfuls were fully present. Here was what Carlo had to say: He and his friend Pasquale were walking down a street in their village in the Abruzzi. They were kicking a small rock and pretending to be Pedro Manfredini, otherwise known as Il Piedone because of the size of his feet, and Humberto Tozzi, two famous Italian footballers from the 1960s who played on opposing teams. Carlo told Pasquale that the supporters of his player's team, Lazio of Rome, were notoriously fascist, and Pasquale retorted that the fans of Roma, where Carlo's allegiance lay, were Burini, dimwits and morons, country bumpkins laced with the aroma of the butter churn. The two boys ended up in a fight. Carlo tore a hole in his new red sweater and his mother had to darn it. The first snow fell. His mother sat by a fire of branches and leaves. At five o'clock the church bell rang and she rose, put on her black shawl, and went to Benediction. The hilltops whitened toward the stars.

When he had finished, it was Tiego's turn. Her brothers were playing football barefoot on the beach with a bunch of friends. A Liberian oil tanker was moored about half a mile offshore. She was watching one boy in particular who moved swiftly and with grace even in the foot-clogging sand. Tiego asked if she could play. The boys as usual said no, but the handsome boy, Antonio, argued for her inclusion. The two of them would be a team and take on everyone else. They played two against six. The sun set behind the Liberian tanker. Whenever they scored a goal Antonio hugged her in celebration (here Carlo spat on the ground). Years later he was imprisoned for distributing antigovernment leaflets. Now he was a telephone repairman in Sierra Leone.

Tiego chucked some peanut shells in the direction of the white bricks. I told them about the time my parents bought me a leather football for my eleventh birthday. I dribbled it through the park to the local London branch library where I had to return a book. The librarian wouldn't let me enter with a muddy ball. I had to leave it outside. I ran in and dropped off the book, *Friday's Tunnel* by John Verney. When I scooted back out the ball had vanished. My parents couldn't afford to replace it.

"Ah, *Poverino,*" said Carlo, miming tears.

We had concluded the football stories and the bottle of grappa.

Because all the stories concerned vanished childhoods, I went straight to the hardware store on Jefferson Street, where substantial objects were placed on solid shelves as a challenge to sentimentality and the longueurs of loss. The shop was open late. There were three peeling, hand-drawn signs in the window: SHADES CUT, LAMPS, and GRASS SEED. Summer business had been terrible, megastores were drawing half the local custom, and the other half was on Martha's Vineyard parasailing or spreading sunblock on their freckled arms. Hence the extended hours set by Edmundos, the owner, an immigrant of ten years' standing from Kaunas in Lithuania.

Oddly enough, my maternal grandparents had left the same town about ninety years earlier, creeping through dark alleys down to an overpriced river barge, then out to the bumpy but liberating Baltic. Wolf and Annie had departed at the urgent behest of local anti-Semites, lightly soused Cossacks, and the conscripting Russian army with its marvelous uniforms and horses but unsporting twenty-five-year shift for Jews. It was thanks to the fortuity of their Western emigration, Kaunas–Rotterdam–London, that I was presently able to share a decent number of leisure hours with my fellow Americans while poor Edmundos, whose family had stayed in place while the boring Soviet Union withered away their lives and their livelihoods, got a late start. As a result, this talented, industrious man was now obliged to work deep into the capitalist night to make an honest three bucks. The god of history was a great joker.

I could see Edmundos's ginger Afro spinning like a tall brush toward the dusty corners of the ceiling. He was on a ladder, adjusting a line of air-conditioning filters. Meanwhile, behind the counter, his loyal sidekick, Joe, took late phone bets on a preseason exhibition football game. Edmundos descended. He was wearing his trademark blue scrub suit. It was on account of this attire that most people in the neighborhood referred to him as "the brain surgeon" while others preferred "the orthodontist." Yet a third group applied the sobriquet "Three Bucks," which I have already inadvertently used, as this was the amount that Edmundos applied to a plethora of miniature items from key chains to wood screws.

In the plumbing corner, sealed off from the rest of the shop by a bosky screen of three tall rubber plants, I placed my bet against Philadelphia to beat the spread, which was seven and a half. The phone rang. It was Carlo, going the other way.

"Money to burn," Joe said, and snapped the gray tongue of the cell phone. Carlo's scratch card accomplishment had led Joe to the opinion that there was little or no justice in the world.

Edmundos swept the floor and hummed a mournful tune—it was like the background music in a black-and-white documentary about Eastern Europe. The words, if they were ever sung, must have gone something like "It's sad to move around from country to country but also sad to stay home." Edmundos had six kids between the ages of two and seventeen. He often asked customers how he was supposed to feed and clothe them and provide them with the necessary American distractions if everybody kept driving out to Home Depot for their duct tape and leaf bags. Nobody ever knew. Once early in the morning I saw Edmundos cruising in his van, lifting five-cent deposit cans from people's recycling bins before the municipal truck arrived.

The rain clouds regrouped and charged once more across the open sky. I drove home. When I came in the door my wife yelled something weighty down the stairs. It sounded like "We need five sacks of coal and a tub of lard."

"Five minutes," I replied.

I sat down in the kitchen and turned on the TV. Somewhere a lame sheep was stuck in muddy pasture; half a mile away a wolf picked up its scent and came bounding in for the kill. The phone rang. It was my sister, calling long distance from London.

"I couldn't sleep," she said, "so I read one of the books that you left behind when you moved to America. It's by someone called Borges. Didn't he write that movie about the postman?"

"I don't think so."

"Never mind that, but tell me something. Aren't there some kind of rules about a short story? Don't they usually go from A to B? Isn't something supposed to happen? Aren't there boundaries?"

She was biting on an apple, maybe a Red Delicious, and I could tell that the snap and flowing juice was hampering her speech.

"I'm sorry," I replied, "I wasn't aware of any rules. But don't take my word for it. I may be wrong."

The TV went to a commercial; rain drummed on the windows. There was an hour to go before kickoff. In the morning I had an appointment at the local hospital, where busy men and women were going to investigate a dull pain that had hibernated in my neck all summer, then woken in my shoulder. I closed my eyes.

Tiego is stroking Carlo's bald head, wringing his wet shirt and admiring his dropsical belly, which puffs out where muscles once lived. "Oh, Carlo," she murmurs, "come let me bathe you in essence of cucumber rose, let me soothe your aches with coconut oil from the flat leeward islands of my homeland, let me sing to you, while you linger in the bath, the songs of the West African coast, where ships berth at Mindelo to scoop up coffee and nuts."

When I awoke, my diesel track of pain had electrified all the way down the line from my head to the ancient seat of emotions in my kidneys. "Night nurse," I called out to no one in particular, "the pain is getting worse."

I came out of the MRI a bit dazed. I had been in the tube for an hour and ten minutes. My wife, bless her, was in the waiting room.

"Oh my God," she said. "Over an hour. You poor guy. Stuck in that coffin with only an inch to breathe. What did you think about?"

I had been thinking about every woman I had ever fucked. It wasn't such a long list, but it had gotten me through. Some women repeated, while others, girls, really, rather than women, appeared around a misty corner after almost thirty years and said "Hi" in the most pleasant way.

"Nothing, really," I replied. "There's a terrible noise in there."

"Nothing? Mind a blank?" she said. "That's not like you. How unusual."

"Death," I said with a sad half smile. "Aneurysm, cancer. I overheard the technician on the phone. 'Soft tissue,' she asked, 'or carotid arteries?'"

My wife shook her head.

"You'll be all right," she affirmed.

I felt all right, sort of. One girl from the memory tube, Jane Furlow, lingered through the long afternoon of waiting for results and on into the early evening. I remembered her up the other end of the bathtub in 1971, the water going cold, her back considerately pushed against the taps. I remembered she was the first girlfriend I ever had who wore a "coil." I remembered her telling me how she was good at only two things: writing poetry and sex—and what a terrible poet she had been—and finally I remembered that she wasn't my girlfriend but somebody else's, a young man called Simon whose job took him to bureaucratic Brussels from time to time. Jane Furlow and I liked each other quite a bit, but in our poorly read early twenties we both believed it was our duty and our fate to suffer in love, so we stuck to our mutually unsuitable partners and saw each other only every six weeks. That went on for two years. Then what happened? I had no idea.

An Ambulance Is on the Way

Dr. Samelson called around eight p.m. with mixed news. My neck appeared to be fine, a few suspicious bone spurs but nothing to get exercised about. On the other hand, the origins of pain were sometimes like the distant mountaintops that sourced the great rivers. He was still concerned. He thought I should see a neurologist. On a lighter note, the heavy rainstorm promised for later in the night was moving out to sea.

"Thanks for the forecast," I said.

Samelson decided to tell me about the best moment of his life. He was fifteen, a skinny guy lacking in self-confidence and friends. It was late spring. He walked across the school yard at dusk under a wild sky studded with clouds, like streptococcal cankers on a pink tongue. The gym was packed. Samelson was wrestling in his weight class for Brookfield High. After a titanic struggle he pinned this other skinny dude from some major wrestling team. Everyone in the building started banging on the wooden seats and yelling his name.

"Thanks, Doc," I said. "You must have been elated."

"You betcha," he replied.

My wife was watching TV and reading a book at the same time. The TV show was a rerun of *Thirtysomething* on Lifetime, the book was *A Life of Picasso,* volume 2, by John Richardson.

"My neck's all right," I said. I was feeling guilty about my torrid memories, so I opted for silence on the subject of the neurologist.

"That's great," my wife replied. "I couldn't live

without you." Despite unusually poor nursing when I am sick with the flu, she really is an excellent person.

When the phone rang again I thought it might be Dr. Samelson calling back with more wrestling stories, but the voice on the other end, low-key and Polish accented, belonged to Willy Gottschalk, my father's first cousin. He was calling my number by mistake. What he wanted was the Veterans Taxi Co., whose listing is a single digit off from my own.

Willy and I had known each other for seven and a half weeks thanks to a happy fact: since the raising of the Iron Curtain, Jews all over the world have been able to trace their roots using the implements of tourist trips to Prague, the records of Eastern European town councils, and skillful Internet surfing. Through the facilitating efforts of my younger sister in London I had become acquainted with the past.

Willy was in Buchenwald, then Colditz, where the Germans ran a mini–concentration camp in the basement, out of sight from the British prisoners of war. After that he was in a DP camp, where he gave a visiting journalist my grandmother's address in London, along with the message that he had survived. Who knows if it ever got through? Then he was in Chicago until a cousin on his wife's side of the family, who was also on his side owing to a little uncle/niece conjugation somewhere down the line, called and invited them to the vast expanse of Texas. For forty-seven years Willy ran a tailor shop in Austin. Then his wife died.

An Ambulance Is on the Way

An octogenarian friend of his from the old country recommended the Boston area as a happy spot for Jewish retirees (was there something wrong with Florida that I didn't know about?). And now here he was domiciled within a mile of my fair suburban home.

The first day we met Willy showed me photos of all my father's first cousins in the Piotrokow ghetto. They were smiling and wearing nice coats because the family were tailors. Everyone had a Star of David armband.

"Why are they smiling?" I asked Willy.

"It was only the first day," he replied.

Here's what I wanted to know: Why hadn't my father ever contacted his Polish cousins? Why hadn't anyone on my side of the family ever said a word about these desperate people, or told the story of their jagged, ruined lives? There was only one person left to ask.

"Mother," I said, transatlantically, "why didn't anyone ever mention Dad's Polish cousins?"

"What Polish cousins?" my mother replied.

I explained the situation.

"Imposters," my mother scoffed. "We're English through and through. Your father, God rest his soul, never had any relatives in continental Europe."

"You must be forgetting," I continued. "Surely you and Dad must have known: the camps, the DP camps, the murdered, the survivors."

"Forgetting? I don't forget anything. Give me one example of something I forget."

"Well," I replied, "if I call you and then I call you again three days later, you don't remember that I've called you the first time."

"When have you ever phoned me three days after you've phoned me the first time? As for these Polish cousins, I tell you again, they're not your relatives. Now, what were you asking me about?"

My mother has Alzheimer's in the muddling middle stage. Things come and go, but mainly go; her short-term memory box is empty. I should never have approached her on this delicate subject in the first place, but I had hoped to steal a thin, warm slice of truth from the charred, inedible pie of reality.

Back in the front room, my wife switched off the TV.

"Are you aware," she asked, "that the squirrels in the roof have chewed two holes in the ceiling of the storage room?"

I was aware, because the last time I entered the storage room, in early April, I had seen one sitting on a suitcase, gnawing the lining of my old down jacket. At the time I simply closed the door and said nothing. It was a rarely used room; spring was arriving in buds and yellow crocus. Surely, without my intervention, Joe Squirrel would reverse paths and inhabit once again his happy summer house in the suburban canopy above the bursting flowers and finely sprinkled lawn.

"Squirrels?" I replied. "You're kidding. In the actual house?"

It was time to sleep.

In the morning, first thing, while my sons were

struggling with their choice of cereal, Eddie the Exterminator came to the door.

"I would have been here earlier," he said, "but my wife had a brain tumor removed on Tuesday, so things are little tough at home."

"Oh my God," I replied.

Eddie held up his fist.

"Size of a grapefruit," he continued, "but benign. Four hours of surgery, two hours in recovery. Can you imagine what she must have been thinking?"

Eddie had the image of a small raccoon embroidered on his overalls, and I thought I saw the animal jump.

"Anyway, never mind our troubles. Your wife called and asked me to go up there"—he pointed skyward—"so I went up there. Here's the problem. The squirrels are leaping onto the roof off the branches of the Norwegian maple, so you need a tree person for the pruning. Then they've eaten through the eaves, so you're going to have to find a carpenter for that, and there's no point in me taking them out until you've completed steps one and two. So what we need here is coordination."

The phone rang. It was Cousin Willy again, asking if I could collect him from his house and take him to the airport.

"I'll be there in half an hour," I said.

"When I call a cab I want it now," he replied. "Why do you think I have an account with you?"

My wife was standing outside with Eddie. Their heads were tilted back. Capricious squirrels scuttled from trunk to runway, then hit an airy flight path from bough to roof. A pair of finches splashed undisturbed in the gutter.

"You should get those leaves from last fall cleaned out," Eddie advised. "That's why the pools are forming."

My sons appeared in heavy slouch formation, exhausted by the hike from kitchen to front door and the five hours of in-class tedium that awaited them.

"Hey, Dad," they said, one in a voice deeper than my own, "we've missed the bus. Give us a ride."

Cousin Willy put his suitcase on the front seat, then sat in the back between the incredible hulks as if they were guarding him.

"It's lucky you came by," he said, "the taxi was late. I was going out of my mind."

We drove in silence until my cantilevered bridge of relatives collapsed in a wild banging of doors outside the school gym; then Willy and I were alone.

"I want to warn you," he began, "that no amount of consideration on your part can make up for your family's indifference to mine during and after the war. A couple of rides to the airport do not compensate for fifty years of silence and neglect."

"Understood," I replied. "Do you want American Airlines or United?"

Willy was flying to Chicago to visit his older brother Louie, a jeweler who in retirement had gone into the gallstone business. Louie was seventy-eight, Willy three years his junior.

We sped down the glistening highway. On one side of the road were giant photographs of all the children who had been shot to death in Boston in the previous year; on the other, spinnakered yachts ran before the wind on choppy black waters.

"United," Cousin Willy replied. "And let me ask you something: Have you read it yet?"

He was referring to "Without Hope," the 2,000-page manuscript with inset photographs that he had dropped on my doorstep almost two months ago: a memoir and manifesto, the Book of Chronicles and the Book of Job, a riot of torn hearts and extirpated souls, the history of a family, my extended, as it turned out, suffering the Nazi mayhem.

I coughed.

"I've finished Chapter One."

The sun came bubbling up over the poster boards like liquid in a lava lamp.

"What is it with your family?" Willy asked. "Half-assed imperviousness to everything that matters. I need an agent, you say you know one. I give you a document that must be published, you stuff it under the bed to gather dust. What's your excuse? You don't have one."

It had been a hard season: close friends had suffered miscarriages and discovered lumps where they weren't supposed to be, one was dying. Then we were broke because of our old-fashioned commitment to art and psychotherapy. Twice, our sons came home with the gift of terrible grades and the promise of professional nullity. On a cold night before dawn the neighborhood bad boys spray-painted expletives on our car and drove their angry fists through the rear window. After that, but not because of it, I experienced the pains that led to the tube and were now about to take me elsewhere.

"Well," Willie continued, "I see you are at a loss for words."

I dropped him at the terminal.

A week later W. Pulone and Sons arrived with their ladders and buzz saws. Soon, lopped branches fell to earth and the tree-bound squirrels, in an anxiety of approach, stepped like nervous swimmers up the narrow, leafy springboards that separated them from their compadres at home. After Pulone came other men with lead plate, tar, and wire mesh. Finally, Eddie appeared with his lures and traps.

"No, no!" I yelled, banging on the kitchen windows and gesturing to the wide outdoors. "Enough."

My sons stood behind me, shoving leeks and long carrots down the garbage disposal to see which vegetable would put up the best fight against its noisy, indefatigable foe.

I ran outside. Eddie's wife was sitting in the front seat of his truck, a wide beehive bandage wound around her head. She was listening to country radio and singing along in a high, cracked voice. Everywhere the warm late-summer air was spliced with noise: the industrious woodpecker at his heavy oak, the gravelly skid of Rollerblades, sixteen-year-olds revving the engines of their mothers' cars, primed for one more high-speed go-round with Lady Luck on the tree-lined boulevards of our treacherous suburb.

"Eddie!" I cried. "Bring down the traps!"

The man on the top of the ladder appeared to sway like a branch in the breeze, but it was only his long, green-shirted arm looping to deposit a metal cage.

"I've already got six," he yelled down. "There's only the mother and her babies left."

"New widows howl, new orphans cry," my wife said, coming up behind me. She is a well-read person with a quote for almost every event.

By nightfall there was no scratching in our roof. My sons rummaged in the storage room for their sports equipment.

"Hey, Dad," they yelled, "there's squirrel shit all over the place. Those little gray bastards chewed the pockets of our lacrosse sticks."

I ignored them and returned to my work desk, where a charge and a responsibility lay like a dull weight on my attenuated Jewish soul. Willy's manuscript was poorly written in broken English. The story, or some version of it, had been told before, ten thousand times: Great-Uncle Velvel hobbling down the Aryan streets at dawn in his mud-spattered bespoke overcoat. The Nazis chasing with knives sharpened for his side locks, behind them baying dogs, then guns, then chimneys. Fast forward to 1997 when America was replete with sensation, spilling over in disclosures and feeling: everyone was pierced, tattooed, overweight, fucking their parents and siblings or humping the family pet. The media outlets were choked with the howls of brutes and their victims, the long wails and high-pitched shrieks of the insulted and the injured.

Cousin Willy was a pain in the ass. I picked up his fat pages and snapped the elastics that held them in place like garters on an old whore's blanched thigh. The agent I knew, Meredith Tobin, specialized in cookbooks, how-to guides, and the autobiographies of recovering alcoholics. "Without Hope" had slept on my rug for forty-nine days. Who was I to disturb its slumber? I thought about chucking it in the garbage, but in the end I slid the manuscript into an oversize bubble envelope, and after breakfast the next morning I drove down to the post office, bought a thick roll of stamps, and mailed that baby off.

A week of summer passed, heavy as the fragrant-tissued elegance of white gardenia on prom night. From Dr. Simcha Ehrlich, a tenant of the seventh-floor neurology unit at Mass General, I received a neck brace, a Swedish pillow, a prescription for the unfashionable drug nortriptyline, a pat on the back, and a "See you next year." The bony outgrowths in my neck were kicking at my nerves like the Lone Ranger's silver spurs into the flanks of Silver, his favorite horse.

Once home, I threw the neck brace into the garbage, then gulped down twice the recommended dose of tablets. After that, I was ready to take the pulse of my patient suburb and shop till I dropped.

An Ambulance Is on the Way

There was a sign stapled to telephone poles all down the street. It read ONE BLACK CAT WITH WHITE PAWS AND CHEST SADLY LOST, and then there was a phone number. It was going to be a hard find. The girls and women of our neighborhood, the suburb's best searchers for lost animals, were bleary-eyed from sleeplessness and weeping. They had all risen in the dark to mourn the hard lives of dumped-on women everywhere by watching Elton John serenade Princess Diana's coffin. Fifty thousand TVs flickered in curtained rooms while WHITE PAWS AND CHEST went her way out from domestic warmth, across the empty roads, and into a wild skunk–stunk, raccoon-rabid feline night.

Where was that darn cat? I couldn't help. I was, by now, on my way home from the market, and carrying two muscle-testing family-size containers of detergent, for there was work to be done. In the purloined space of my hypochondriacal summer I had developed an enthusiasm for laundry: separating, tough decisions about what constitutes dark, choice of cleansing agent (I always went with clear), adjustments to length of wash, different cycles of drying, the efficacy of finish guard, folding. The hard part was putting away. The female in my house, unlike the males, who played things as they lay, preferred the ordered secrecy of drawers and closets. I couldn't let her down. In the process of my domestic education I was learning what every woman already knew, and not only about laundry. I culled esoteric, gender-specific information, such as how sticks of butter feature wrapper markings that

79

are measures for baking, or the difference between the bundt pan and the springform pan.

When you are into something you tend to chat about it, and then, whether the topic is sex or laundry or Princess Di, you find out all kinds of things. For example, my sister-in-law told me that she loved to fold laundry while watching soaps on TV, while Liz, our next-door neighbor, had been bowled over since childhood by the aromas of fresh sheets and pillowcases. Then there's the minuet with their mothers that everyone remembers, stepping back with a stretched white sheet, two folds and a two-step forward. The pleasure of drudgery is something that most politically inclined individuals seem to have missed.

After a week of time-sharing with other members of my family I assumed total control of the wash 'n' dry area. I went a little crazy and became the Lady Macbeth of laundry, dousing and cleansing everything I could get my hands on, including the heavy bathroom rugs that upset the balance of the machine and sent it staggering across the floor in a noisy, lumbering four-footed dance, like an appliance in a Disney spectacular.

Inevitably, as with our treacherous bodies, my excesses led to damage. The lid broke on the washing machine and shortly after a chimney full of lint blocked the air duct from the dryer: but these events were simple warnings, tremors, tests, preparations for fire and flood. Soon there came a spark that short-circuited the dryer, and shortly after that the Whirlpool churned, spilled its banks, ran the levee of piled clothes on the floor, and turned the basement into a paddy field.

As a book-loving, although not bookish, adolescent in the exciting mid-sixties, I had read in James Joyce's *Portrait of the Artist as a Young Man* that by thinking about things you could understand them. The instruction, like little else from that time, had stuck with me. So I stood ankle-deep in water and mentally engaged the machines. My mind drew a blank.

"Sad about your princess," Albert said. His bald pate shone from beneath the sink, where he was struggling with a wrench and a resistant bolt. "My wife and daughter got up at four."

It seemed like a moment for expanded solidarity, so I replied, "Mine too," although I didn't have a daughter.

"I watched the rerun at eight."

Again, I concurred.

"What about that Charles? He should fight Tyson— give Mike something he could really chew on."

Albert began to hum. As accompaniment he banged out rough music on the pipes and groaned occasionally like Keith Jarrett at the piano. I watched in a state of interested awkwardness, which is familiar to all who live in a world that they can govern briefly but never fix.

I wanted to leave. I had a late-morning appointment at Tone-Up Massage with the dextrous Rochelle Shavinsky, who at the height of the border war between Armenia and Azerbaijan had, in the company of her earnest, computer-skilled husband, Yefim, transported her impressive ability to relieve muscle ache all the way from Baku to Brookline. In the early months of my neck pain my brother-in-law, Arnie Strom, had provided me with a gift certificate to Rochelle's highly recommended and aboveboard establishment. I had cashed in the winning ticket weeks ago and fallen into the perfumed bath of self-indulgence. Now I was hooked. Worse, every visit to Tone-Up was tinged with the feeble remorse that attaches to wasted years. I could have been a long-term regular in a hands-on environment; instead, my ethnic affiliation and comfortable median spot in the class system had led me to the drain of psychotherapy, down which I had poured the contents of my soul and a thousand wallets.

"Can I get a bucket?" Albert lay supine on the soaked rug. He was about to open the sluice gates. I passed him a red plastic pail shaped and colored exactly like the one that, as a small child, I used to fill with tap water and drag into my backyard on hot summer days in lieu of a swimming pool. For a moment the branches of a plum tree swayed and beckoned above my head, and then I was back in the basement with Albert and the rising damp.

I went upstairs. My wife was in the kitchen with Mahdavi Basu, one of her book-group friends. The morning papers were spread out before them. They were on a break between phone calls: women in an ever-widening radius had been calling to grieve and vent. From Asia to Australia there was a global production of *Lysistrata*. The princess, with her aristocratic lineage, movie-star beauty, constructed self-exposure, shopping extravaganzas, and bags of money, was suddenly Everywoman, fucked over by a jerk and trying her best to grab five minutes of love and peace.

"Hi," I said.

My wife and Mahdavi looked at me as if I were the royal tampon on his way back from a liaison with Camilla.

It seemed as though it might be a good morning for guys to get out of town.

"Where are you off to?" my wife asked, noting something in my body language that suggested imminent departure.

"Tone-Up," I muttered sorrowfully, as if I was saying "the dentist."

Mahdavi began to list the princess's selfless accomplishments, all the causes that she had worked for or fronted: the Red Cross, AIDS patients, land mine victims in Bosnia.

I was humbled. My own acts of public charity were limited to bags of clothes for Vietnam vets, an annual ten-dollar check to the local firemen's ball, and, in a moment of false consciousness, twenty-five big ones to the Jewish National Fund, which, it turned out, had not gone to help plant cypress saplings in the scorching desert but down into the rich earth that lined the pockets of executive fat cats. In any case, an hour at Tone-Up suddenly required a different plea: not temporary indulgence but terminal narcissism. On the other hand, the princess herself had enjoyed the rigors of step aerobics and personal training.

I drove down shaded streets, then pulled in for gas at the Walnut Shell station, run for the last eight years by two Syrian brothers, Sami and Ghassan. My cousin Deirdre had once let Sami kiss her on the cheek. "When are you going to go out with me?" he'd kept asking her, holding on to her debit card as if it were a kidnapped child. "I can't stand it." One sultry afternoon, as the temperature climbed toward ninety and the pump whirred with gallons and dollars like a Vegas slot in heat, Deirdre leaned out the window of her Toyota Camry and said, "Plant one here and be done." "It was strange," she told me afterward, "because I actually like the other brother, the one with the mustache."

At Tone-Up there was a sign and two photographs taped to the glass door. The black-bordered felt-tip lettering said IN MOURNING. CLOSED. The pictures, set above and below the sign, were of Princess Diana (above) and the family of the long deceased Romanov Czar Nicholas II (below), a group portrait with an arrow pointing to Princess Anastasia.

Out of the corner of my eye I spotted Rochelle Shavinsky emerge from Celtic Crust, cradling a Styrofoam cup. When I turned to face her I saw that her eyes were red from crying.

"Like a candle in the wind," she said in her furry Russian accent, extending an arm and then extinguishing an imaginary flame with moist, pursed lips. "I'm sorry," she added. "I cannot touch a man today."

We sat on a long bench flanked by a blue newspaper dispenser and a concrete municipal wastebasket. Behind us the suburban surf of Sunday morning traffic washed up from the rippling highway.

"In Baku, when I was teenager," Rochelle began, "I wore ankle bracelets with small silver bells. My father liked them but my mother thought they made me look like a whore."

The sun hid behind a cloud. Rochelle sipped her coffee and sighed. Seven winters moved across the steppes.

"So what's your problem?" she asked finally.

"Neck pains."

She stood up, maneuvered behind the bench, and absentmindedly began to massage, digging her fingers deep into my flesh, her promise to abjure men subdued by the exigencies of the masseuse's Hippocratic oath.

"Ah, Dodi," she murmured. "Why so fast?"

There are betrayals everywhere.

It was while we were thus engaged that I thought I saw WHITE PAWS AND CHEST testing all nine lives at once among the killer cars that ran the blinking amber light outside Debbie's Petland and Aquarium. Before I had a chance to do anything, the lost kitty, or her patchy doppelgänger, had disappeared around a corner.

It is a truth universally acknowledged that people

who have time on their hands sleep more than they ought to, and I was no exception to this rule. In the waning morning I catnapped on the bench like the clochards of old, while Ms. Shavinsky headed home to tell her husband to cook his own stroganoff.

By the time I returned to my own domicile there were three TVs going but no one there to watch them. I was itching to do some laundry, a chore and an entertainment that the late princess had probably never known, and now, sadly, the opportunity was lost to her forever. Unfortunately, Albert had left his work half done. I found fleeting solace in seeing that the lint tray was full and required the sweep of a licked forefinger to clear, but I had been after the full monty: the first turbulent swishes of a loaded machine, light angled in arrow shafts across the white enamel surface of the dryer, an errant sock snatched up and deposited in already foaming water, the lid slamming tinnily on a job well done.

Hours passed. I went out to the deck. In the stop-time of my backyard, hydrangeas hung their late-summer mauves and whites along a line of bushes. In the adjacent garden my neighbors, who had lost their son to cancer three months earlier, were planting a rose of Sharon. They dug awhile, then leaned on their shovels, as if to be propped up.

One by one the members of my family returned home and retreated to their rooms. In the confusions of summer and the apprehension of loss I was up all night, until the first quiet and pure light of day received a thud and slide of two newspapers in blue plastic wrap. In the kitchen where I had been sitting, I took a peach from the fruit bowl and bit. From the press of my fingers I had imagined it was going to be soft and full of juice, but it turned out to be hard and inedible. I determined to go out and look for that cat.

I searched all through the day in the leafy grounds of that huge convalescent home, the world. More specifically I roamed my fat lost-cat suburb, a place where everybody I knew was recovering from something: the rocks and hard places of modern life. I'm talking about divorce, the sicknesses of relatives or selves, deaths of loved ones, moral and financial bankruptcies, alcoholism, drug abuse, and down in the adolescent precincts of broken hearts and the side effects of Ecstasy.

As I meandered like a lost seagull in the wake of a slow-moving orange Pelican truck that simultaneously brushed and wetted the street, I pondered a problem that went as follows: What message had I sent into the electronic night a week ago that, shortly after breakfast this morning, had elicited the following reply from my friend B. in Hawaii: "Whew!!! No Thanks!"? What preposterous offer of mine had first taken his breath away, then lead to an emphatic decline? I used to think that memory loss was middle age's gift to overburdened consciousness, but now I wasn't so sure. I could call B.

and ask him, of course, but B. was unreliable in all areas apart from carpentry. He had been an indiscreet boozer for twenty-one years, ever since, so he said, he had become emotional during the Bicentennial. His saw hand remained steady, but everything else was on the wobble.

By late in the day I was still out on the street, not so much on behalf of the stray, but because my wife's object group was coming over; the unusual name was a response to the failure of her book group. Who reads books anymore? Even the intelligent women of our neighborhood have given up. By a vote of nine to one they decided to look at meaningful things instead: a toolbox that had belonged to somebody's grandfather in Odessa, lace tablecloths, old shoes, all manner of items that over the years had gotten tangled in their hearts and minds, like driftwood. It was show-and-tell for grown-ups. They loved it.

On this soft summer evening I was asked to help. My mission was to buy French bread, low-fat cheese, and wine (red, of course, for the heart): the bourgeois staples of a successful soiree at home under the stars and deck lights with the citronella candles all aglow, the kitchen mealy moths trapped by glue in their Pherecon tepees.

On the corner of Beacon Street, two blocks from Bread and Circus supermarket, Iris Steinsaltz stopped her curvaceous Ford Taurus when she saw me and downed its electronic window to complain about my youngest son's cruelty to hers. She spoke mildly, because we were in the "use your words" suburbs, but with emphasis, in case I missed her point. In some shadowy recess of the Frank Klopas School playground, while the eleven-year-old girls swung on metal poles like strippers in training, my Sam had told Iris's Marco that he was, unequivocally, "the worst athlete in the world." Marco, his fragile ego cradled like a robin's egg in Iris's smooth hands, had been rushed into therapy, where the egg was gently inflated via the thin straw and hushed breath of the talking cure in seven fifty-minute sessions.

Ten feet from Iris's front wheels, a crow was davening into the entrails of a roadkill squirrel.

I grabbed Iris's arm and gave it an Indian burn. No, I didn't. I stared at her smug, kvetchy face and said: "Well, if those boys are going to remain friends, they must learn to be kinder to each other."

Tolerance is supremely respected in our town, like vitamin E and side-door air bags, so Iris had nowhere to go from my measured response, except on toward the market, with its ripe horned melons and succulent passion fruit. I followed at the vagrant's pace that fits both my employment situation and my general state of mind.

I marched past the hi-glow organic tomatoes in the direction of low-fat cottage cheese. I was swinging my basket like Red Riding Hood and stepping in sprightly fashion. I was full of life-affirming forces and bonhomie on account of the other e-mail I had received that morning, which was erotic in nature and came from my wife. She was making me an offer I couldn't refuse. All I had to do was wait for the object group to leave.

On my way home I stopped by the summer season's last Little League game. The lights on the electronic scoreboard donated by Ronnie's Luncheonette glowed pleasantly in the approaching dusk, shadows gathered and lengthened in the deep fields, and dark chestnuts overhung the players' benches exactly as they are supposed to. Feeling an antisocial force lurch inside me, I roughly debagged the wine intended for the object group, uncorked it with my Swiss Army knife, and took a swig.

Auburn-haired Mike Marshall, the coach's son, tall and broad-shouldered before his time, was on the mound, and dark George Lustiger at the plate. My own progeny occupied a lonely spot at the far end of an otherwise vacant aluminum bench. His head was concentratedly down while he inscribed Caucasian circles in white dust with the toes of his cleats.

Through the medium of troubled conversation over tall skim lattes at Starbucks, the sighs and sobs that are the afternoon talk show of the suburbs, I was familiar with the medical and educational records of most adults and children in our neighborhood. I happened to know, for example, that George's mother had recently undergone a hysterectomy, although there was a feeling in some quarters that the procedure had been unnecessary. I knew too that Mike Marshall's brother Harry was diabetic, and that Mike himself was considered by his psychologist but not by his teachers (who saw a behavior problem) to possess the mercurial distractions of an ADD sufferer.

The pitches came flying in like miniature versions of the asteroids that will one day destroy us all. The day's last white clouds scudded in from the west. Sam produced a yo-yo from his pocket and sent it spinning. My mind started to drift. At about twelve-thirty a.m., by my calculations, after the last object had returned to the mundane vehicle of its arrival—bag or box—and the last object group member to her car, I would lie with my wife under a moonstruck square of window, and, while the neighbor's brown Labrador howled at a tree-bound raccoon, we would remind each other that on their curious journey through middle age toward the millennium, bodies at night sometimes need motion as well as rest.

Is there a more powerful deus ex machina in the modern world than the adaptable cell phone? Two blips and I was homeward bound, the dark grapes of Burgundy staining my lips with lies in ready explanation of the uncorked wine.

"I was thirsty and it was your world," I said to my wife, who was setting a sun-dried tomato dip in the volcanic orifice of a pile of crackers.

She glanced at the half-empty bottle.

"Are you going to be here for this event, or are you going out?" she replied.

On the shelf behind her left elbow, beside a mirror fractured by the day's last burning light, sat a bowl of peaches and a pile of unread books. My wife had placed a thin vase of yellow freesias on Mia Farrow's face.

"I'll be gone by the time they get here," I replied. "Don't worry."

I deposited the wine in the kitchen and went upstairs. For about a half an hour I surfed the World Wide Web in search of pornography. As usual EaRos and Erotica Tender were mysteriously inaccessible to me, as was the Web site of Red Hot Amsterdam. I was forced to settle for Tantric Amour, clued to the needs of corporate lovers "with little time or changing schedules." Eventually, a profiled breast with the nipple more or less indistinguishable surrendered to the keys and applied for cheap, fuzzy admission on the screen.

I went out.

It took me about fifteen minutes to get to Blockbuster. My cousin Deirdre was sitting adjacent to the entrance on a bench outside Ice Cream Works. She was licking a Cool Cow ten-calories-per-ounce chocolate yogurette and looking miserable.

"What's the matter?" I asked. I could tell she was going to press me for an opinion on the size of her ass. She had done so the last time we met by chance. She assumes that because we have known each other since childhood I will provide the honest answer that her husband withholds. It took about five minutes of chat before she got up the nerve, but then she went for it:

"Is my ass too big?"

As a general rule I try not to disappoint people with whom I have a close relationship, but recently I have lost a measure of the charm and delicacy that I once possessed. So I replied, "It's not huge."

My cousin gazed down the block in the direction of a stationary red eighteen-wheeler. Two men in overalls were unloading office supplies onto a dolly.

"Thanks a lot." She was swallowing gravel.

I went inside and rented *Marathon Man*. It was one of those movies that I always thought I wanted to see again, but didn't really.

"Die weisse Engel," my cousin said in a sad voice when she saw what I was holding in my hand. Then she sighed. I didn't know if she was thinking about the Holocaust or the size of her ass. It was an awkward situation.

I took the scenic route home via the old aqueduct, around the back of a cluster of cottages where young first-home buyers lived. There were piles of aromatic wood chips, like small burial mounds, all along the trodden path, and blue and white wildflowers in front of the fences. Birds wheeled above the tree line, flapping their wings with a remote sound of applause. I saw a couple of kids on a swing set, one daring the other to jump from an enormous, leg-breaking height. Dusk was lowering its dim orange curtain, changing the scenery behind my back. I could still feel the effects of the wine that I had drunk. A pig in his liquid trough.

By the time I returned home the object group had assembled. Seven suburban gypsies with long earrings were gathered around our coffee table, their wares spread before them on a rose-patterned tablecloth.

I took two steps into the room.

"And pat he comes," my wife announced, "like the Catastrophe of the Old Comedy."

The gypsies looked up. I could tell that they weren't pleased with me. Because of my premature guzzling the meniscus sat low in each of their wineglasses, an orbit of disappointed red crescent moons.

"We were discussing gorillas," Judy Pfizer said, "and the sad dark secret of their species."

"Which is?" I asked.

"For all his muscle even the much-feared silverback sports a penis only one and a half inches in length."

On the table lay an image of the speaker's bearded and bare-chested first husband. I knew this man—we had played music together as parental backups to the band during last fall's middle school production of *Anything Goes*. Months later he had lap-danced his way out of marriage and into an AIDS test. I looked around the group, and each woman, I now noticed, had, squared neatly before her, a photograph that displayed an object of former affection now offered as an object of scorn. Or perhaps that was true in only some cases. Was it love and loss in the others?

"What a dick that man was," Judy Pfizer continued, pushing the photo into a neutral zone beyond her own space on the table.

"Sounds like a total prick," added a woman I had never met before. The accent was British.

The insults came fast and deadly, like small bursts of fire from a Kalashnikov rifle. It occurred to me that only certain euphemisms for *penis* could be used against their owners: for example, you couldn't apply *Johnson* or *pecker* in a derogatory manner. No one said "He was a total Johnson" or "a complete pecker." Why was this? I swiftly appraised the room's collective mood and decided not to ask. Instead, I craned my neck to see who my wife was presenting. With a mixture of relief and disappointment I saw before her not my face but that of James Leviathan, the fiancé who had punched her father in the nose back in 1972 during an argument about the pluses and minuses of LSD.

Sam came in the door behind me.

"We lost," he said, and trudged upstairs.

I followed him into his room, where he sat disconsolately on the bed. I was going to make a familiar uplifting speech about what truly mattered in life, but Sam anticipated my dull intention and cut me off.

"It's all right," he said. "I'm in the yo-yo club."

"What's that?"

"You have to know three tricks to get in."

He stood up and produced the toy. The string flew out and in; the translucent red disk twirled, danced, crept, and slept. Sam walked the dog, went round the world, and cat's-cradled the yo-yo. I retreated forty years. A whole morning from my childhood rose and fell. I was in a weak, constricted time, the yo-yo running its string in a bleak hospital corridor. Inside an adjacent room my father sat in a transparent oxygen tent waiting for death (which knew more than three tricks) to steal through his striped flannel pajamas.

95

Beyond his thinly curtained windows were clouds and dim stars.

There was laughter from the object group below and the clink of coffee cups on saucers. A couple hours later my wife came up to bed. Before long, we were naked and not too ashamed. The scent of peach juice was on her fingers, and, for the first time in months, the pain in my neck had miraculously disappeared. I made a decision to side with life.

"How about," I asked, "if I don't use a condom?"

"Whew!" my wife replied. "No thanks!"

Lothar
and
Inez

Lothar Mermelstein was traveling from New York to Madrid via Paris. It was the fifth year since his retirement from Cedars-Sinai, where he had set up and administered the cardiac unit back in the ignorant early sixties, when *bypass* was still a highway term and digitalis the remedy of choice for patients with malfunctioning valves.

He was a small man with an obviously intelligent face and long white hair scooped back "genius-style." He had worn a cream suit to travel, and there was only the soupçon of a burgher's belly above his belt to indicate how well he had lived for the last two decades.

He watched his wife settle their hand luggage into the overhead compartment, let her through into the window seat, then settled down and buckled his seat belt. The point of the journey was to see old friends in France, then replay the trip south that he and Inez had taken on their European honeymoon almost forty years earlier, when he had brought her to see the house in which he had spent a part of his childhood and teenage years. Inez was nineteen when they had met, the daughter of one of Lothar's patients, and he, already a highly respected figure at Cedars-Sinai, had just turned thirty-five.

The stewardesses did their thing. As it was an Air France flight, Mermelstein spoke to them in French, moving happily into the language, speaking confidently and courteously. To his wife, he spoke, as he always preferred to, in Spanish.

The young man sitting on his other side, whose name was David and who had himself recently turned thirty-five, observed the Mermelsteins with interest. He was already infatuated with the wife before she spoke in Spanish, and when she did so something very close to passion began to burn in his impressionable heart. David, who loved the novels of Gabriel García Márquez, imagined that the woman's name was Mercedes or perhaps Fermina. He would have been disappointed to learn that Inez, who was indeed a woman of great beauty, with long, thick black hair and deep brown eyes, hailed from Puerto Rico rather than one of the more exotic countries in Central or South America.

Back in 1957, at first sight, Mermelstein had fallen in love with a woman who was a mere sixteen years younger than he. Fast-forward four decades and David was experiencing an almost identical sense of over-whelming love for a woman twenty-four years his se-nior. It should be said that this was not entirely a bolt from the blue. It had been several months since older women had begun to swing into his sexual purview. At the supermarket he found himself looking down a wider range of open blouses than had ever attracted him before. Obviously it was nature's way: older mem-bers of the other sex becoming increasingly attractive as you yourself aged, although, interestingly, the young ones never ceased to be appealing.

David, a high school teacher by profession, was on the way to Paris because his first book of stories, which had been moderately well received in the United States, was about to appear in a French translation. No one had invited him to France, and his publishers there, Arte-Sud, had expressed no interest in meeting him. Never-theless, he thought it would be fun to see his books in a foreign bookstore. Since he was always on the look-out for new material, the sudden eruption of his feel-ings for Inez Mermelstein, the cosmopolitan affect of her husband, and the excitements of travel all com-bined to form a web of inspiration. David, before any-thing more than the mildest pleasantries had passed between himself and his fellow travelers, was already imagining a story.

When the FASTEN SEAT BELT sign flashed off Lothar removed his jacket, loosened his tie, and set his seat back. He was then ready to begin a conversation, and he began by asking David, who was reading the *New*

York Review of Books, if he was familiar with the works of Thomas Mann. David was, and Mermelstein went on to describe the plot of one of his favorite stories, "Mario the Magician." From this he proceeded to a discussion of Dostoevsky and from thence to Kafka and on to Sartre, whom Mermelstein had known in Paris in the immediate postwar years when writers were easily approachable at their favorite Left Bank cafés.

David was terribly excited to be having this conversation with someone who appeared to be a genuine European intellectual of the Old School. He imagined that Mermelstein must be a professor of comparative literature, probably at Columbia rather than NYU. His wife, he guessed, must be one of his former students, or possibly a younger colleague. Mrs. Mermelstein, or Mercedes (David had decided on Mercedes), was sitting up with her eyes closed, and it was with her eyes closed that she undid the top two buttons on her black cashmere cardigan. Had her eyes been open the gesture would still have affected David and sent his heart racing, but their being closed made the subsequent exposure of her cleavage and a line of black brassiere even more exciting.

The evening meal was served, and Mermelstein, while pouring his wine, gently scolded David for not speaking French to the stewardess. By this time David had learned that Mermelstein was not an English professor but *the* Lothar Mermelstein, one of the world's most renowned heart surgeons, a figure on a par with Bernard Lown or Israel Seymour, for these were the men whom Lothar had accompanied on the 1995 trip to Moscow that he was now describing so vividly to David. Mermelstein, of course, understood Russian and had been able to catch the muttered asides of the nurses that so powerfully contradicted the bullshit the visitors were being handed by the hospital functionaries and senior doctors.

Mermelstein did not say so, but David thought he remembered that this same Mermelstein was in fact a Nobel Prize winner. Over coffee Lothar told him how he had begun his education as a student of philosophy, switching to medicine only in his twenties and in response to pressure from his father, who was himself a doctor. "Use your mind to help others," his father had said.

Lothar, it turned out, had known not only Sartre but also Camus. David and Lothar agreed that Sartre was the better thinker but Camus the better novelist. In Paris, and later in New York, Mermelstein had mixed with various groups of writers and intellectuals. He had also, as an impetuous young man, once argued with Einstein over the existence of God. Einstein being for, of course, and he, Lothar, against—as he still was.

David was thrilled. He considered it an enormous stroke of luck to have landed next to this brilliant man and his beautiful wife. There could be no doubt that Dr. Mermelstein was an authentic personality: everything about him bespoke honesty and truth. It was a privilege simply to listen to the man talk. And there was nothing pompous, or pretentious, or egotistic in his conversation. Naturally, David wanted to show Mermelstein his own book, but he held himself in check, not wanting to appear self-aggrandizing. In the presence of someone who had known Einstein and Sartre, modesty was the best policy. This was confirmed when, after the third or fourth quote that Mermelstein had asked David to identify, "Mercedes" leaned over her husband and whispered conspiratorially, "He likes to test people." David smiled, but inside he felt as if she had tipped her tongue with honey and thrust it into his mouth. That accent! That hair! And where he hadn't dared to let his eyes roam as she bent forward, those breasts held in that simple black bra!

Lothar was enjoying himself. He had already told the young man, whose name he could not remember and who must have been about the same age as his own oldest son, Alberto, who was thirty-five and the public relations officer for a dance company in New York, his pet theory concerning heart disease. It was an idea he had developed in the last two years when he had become convinced that the cause of heart problems was fundamentally bacterial. It was, he knew, a radical notion, but as with, say, the recent discovery, a surprise to all, that ulcers were bacterial in cause and could easily be cleared up through the administering of antibiotics, so too, Mermelstein was convinced, would it go with heart disease. The young man had asked him why the Masai, whose tribal life he had followed in a TV documentary, had not recorded a single instance of death through heart attack, and Mermelstein had replied that in all probability, and especially as the Masai "ate all the wrong things—milk, milk, and milk!," the tribe had not yet been exposed to whatever the bacteria was that caused all the trouble! Stress, of course, made one vulnerable to attack, and so indeed it was true that stress, indirectly, was the cause of many deaths. And yet almost all the bypasses performed in the United States were, in Mermelstein's opinion, unnecessary. Most of the sickness could be dealt with through the reduction of stress.

The plane sped through the night. "Mercedes" slept again. She wore the mask provided by the airline but not the slipper socks. The mask, in black faux silk, repeated the motif of her underwear. David wanted to kiss her on the lips. Instead he began to watch the movie, but only one side of his headphones functioned properly and he soon gave up.

In time all three fell asleep. But Inez was not asleep; she was merely drowsing. A number of thoughts were preoccupying her and returning with greater and lesser intensity. First, she was worried about the long drive from Paris to Madrid. Ever since his retirement, as if to decrease the amount of time that he wasted, or perhaps to demonstrate that his reactions were as sharp as a working man's, Lothar had taken to driving very fast. For a man of seventy-five he was picking up an inordinate number of speeding tickets. America's highways were broad, well policed, and governed by a strict and low limit. In Europe Lothar would be free to indulge his unfortunate habit. In the dark tube of the plane, which felt motionless, Inez pictured herself hurtling toward Nice, her hand on the door's grip, where, when she was driving alone, she normally hung dry cleaning. Second, she was thinking about Dr. Emanuel Moses, Lothar's old friend in whose apartment they were going to spend three nights in Paris. Dr. Moses and his wife lived close to the fruit and vegetable market on the rue Mouffetard. In the first year of her marriage to Lothar, Inez had almost had an affair with Emanuel. In fact, one hot July afternoon when Lothar was attending a conference in San Diego, she and Emanuel had gotten so far as to lie topless together on a couch in the front room of his apartment on West 110th Street. At a distance of almost forty years, she could still feel the touch of his hand on her breast and she could still hear the ring of the doorbell that they had not answered but that had brought Inez back to her senses. It now seemed to her that the interruption was for the best: her long friendship with Emanuel, and with his wife, Millie, would not have been possible if she had slept with him. Lastly, Inez was concerned about the cystitis from which she had been suffering for the last week or so. Her discomfort made journeys like this especially difficult, and, in fact, had Lothar not seemed so eager to travel she would have tried harder to persuade him to stay home.

As Inez finally fell into a light sleep, David awoke. He rose from his aisle seat and joined the short line outside the bathroom. He glanced back at his sleeping companions. Dr. Mermelstein's personal history was a puzzle. If he had grown up in Spain, why did he have both a German accent and a German name? For a moment the ugly thought flashed through David's mind that Lothar was a former Nazi, a postwar braindrainer with a past, like some of the scientists whom the Americans had picked up for the space program.

But the chronology was all wrong. If Lothar was seventy-five, then he must have been born in 1922. But what was his family doing in Madrid? Perhaps he had met the beautiful "Mercedes" there. She was the daughter of a family close to the Mermelsteins. He had known her as a small child when he was already in his teens. Years later they had met up again in New York. Now she was a grown-up beauty!

David found the bathroom in a barely acceptable mid-flight state; soon it would be unusable. The soap had been crushed into the bowl and its wrappers left on the floor next to a streamer of damp toilet paper.

After peeing David splashed water on his face. He wished that he had brought his toothbrush in with him. It would be nice to have fresh breath in the event, highly unlikely he knew, that it would be he and not Dr. Mermelstein who found himself in bed with "Mercedes" on their first night in Paris.

David returned to his seat. He pressed on his reading light, flipped through the pages of a magazine, pressed the light off again, and slept deeply.

He was awoken by Inez, who was violently shaking his left shoulder.

"Do something! Do something!"

Dr. Mermelstein had pitched forward in his seat and was emitting a series of strangulated moans. His forehead was clammy and his face a pale shade of purple.

David had no idea what to do. The thought flashed through his mind that the previous three hours of conversation had been the old doctor's way of preparing his neophyte companion for just such an event. Between Kennedy and the mid-Atlantic, Mermelstein had taught David everything he knew, and now it was incumbent upon David to save him. "Nurse, gloves and scalpel, please. This is simply a case of bacterial infection and stress." David was ready. The corollary to his readiness was, of course, the enormous gratitude of "Mercedes."

David rose from his seat to fetch a stewardess. Outwardly, be began to behave as helpfully and altruistically as he could, although he was severely limited in what he could do by a complete ignorance of first-aid procedures. Nevertheless, he did manage to raise the chair arm that had formerly separated him from the doctor and generously relinquish his seat to the now sprawling Dr. Mermelstein. Inwardly, and shamelessly, David could not help but entertain the most depraved fantasies. In terms of his passion for "Mercedes," Dr. Mermelstein's potentially mortal sickness was more than fortuitous; it was necessary. David was not a silly person. Indeed, he was known as a charismatic and creative but responsible twelfth-grade teacher, and his stories had been praised for their maturity and sensitivity. Nevertheless, like all people, he was vulnerable to inappropriate thoughts, which passed through his mind with the regularity and reliability of a German train.

Inez, after shouting for help, was busy loosening Lothar's tie and undoing the top buttons of his shirt, which revealed a sprig of white mattress stuffing that was the carnal opposite of her own bosom. Inez held Lothar's hand and whispered to him in Spanish, and then she let go of his hand, stroked his face, and murmured in English, "Don't die."

Lothar Mermelstein was, at this point, the only person on the plane who knew that he was not having a heart attack. Although he had briefly lost his breath and was certainly overheated, he did not anticipate his immediate demise. If he could only regain his breath, he would be able to tell everybody what to do. As it was, he found himself confined to the loving ministrations of his wife and the gathering concern of fools and imbeciles.

In response to the assistant pilot's broadcast request for medical assistance, *"Est ce qu'il y a un médecin à bord,"* a small crowd had now congregated in the aisle. A bearded middle-aged American academic, Harry Pfeiffer, who had been eyeing one of the slim French stewardesses more or less since takeoff, now saw an opportunity to approach her.

"I'm a doctor," he said with a smile, "but not a medical doctor."

It was true. Harry had a Ph.D. in sociology and in fact was on his way to a conference at the University of Paris in Nanterre.

Harry's remark was so crass, so out of place and unseemly, so foolish and heartless, such a mistaken reading of the situation, that, despite the well-known link between the excitements of near-death experiences and sexual rushes, no one saw fit to register it in their consciousness, let alone respond. Except for David, who felt an odd moment of jealousy. If anyone was the doctor-who-was-not-really-a-doctor, then surely it was he. Who was this imposter?

The stewardesses rustled and flapped. Their faces showed both grave concern and irritation. The last thing they wanted was a corpse on board. *"Où est un médecin?"* they repeated, until with a great effort Lothar roused himself to rasp:

"Moi! Je suis le médecin. Le médecin, c'est moi!"

David stood squeezed between a stewardess's nicely shaped backside and the duty-free tray. Despite the provocation, he still maintained his allegiance to fifty-nine-year-old "Mercedes," a devotion that was heightened by her astonishing display of passionate concern for her husband. Inez acted exactly how David would have wanted her to had he written her scene himself. Her hair flew, her bosom heaved, her cries were loud, her sobs excessive, and her demands that someone help her husband grew relentlessly histrionic.

In the end, Dr. Mermelstein helped himself. He

pressed his right hand to his forehead and gazed at the watch on his left wrist: in this way he took his pulse. It was low. He asked for, and received, a small oxygen tank, from which he regulated his own intake. He then instructed Inez to help lift him, and the two of them disappeared into one of the cramped bathrooms. When they returned Dr. Mermelstein still looked to everyone else as if he was at death's door, but he declared himself to be on the quick road to full recovery.

As Lothar rested in his chair, Inez turned her attention to David. She thanked him profusely and exorbitantly for his help. David, who had done absolutely nothing except rise from his chair, intercept a stewardess, and imagine her husband dead, waved away her gratitude with a sheepish smile.

For the next hour David sat directly behind Lothar in a seat that had been vacated by a priest who preferred to stand at the back of the plane. When the doctor was clearly himself again, Inez turned around and requested that David retake his original position.

Lothar lay with his head back and his eyes closed. He was thinking about Madrid, the city to which his parents had brought him in 1933. Lothar, who was eleven at the time, remembered very little about the journey from Germany, but he vividly recalled the table setting for breakfast on the first morning after the family's arrival, the way the sun appeared to rise from the table and the plates revolved beautifully in a pattern of lemons.

The picture in Dr. Mermelstein's mind was precisely the kind of image that would have delighted David, had he only known of its existence.

The closer they got to Paris, the more reality and the inevitability of David's separation from "Mercedes" asserted themselves. By the time the shutters on the windows were lifted and the gray, rainy morning announced itself, David was not even sure that "Mercedes" was beautiful. Although, in fact, she was.

It was while he was stretching up to retrieve the Mermelsteins' hand luggage that David first heard Lothar address his wife as "Inez." David had to resist an impulse to correct him. The two men did not exchange addresses or phone numbers, but, like most air travelers, they simply said a warm good-bye and hoped to avoid the embarrassment of seeing each other again in close proximity at the baggage claim, where a second and lamer farewell would be required. As they were parting, David could not resist reminding Lothar that he, David, was a published author.

"Well," he said, "you certainly gave me a good story."

Lothar's response was not what David was hoping for. For a start, he did not smile, and David immediately felt that Lothar knew everything that he had been thinking throughout the flight. He knew, in other words, that David had dreamed him dead and imagined himself in bed with his wife.

"A good story, yes," Lothar finally said. "But it had better have a happy ending."

David understood this remark as a warning. Lothar, who had plenty of life left in him, did not wish to undergo a fictional murder.

For three days in Paris, David dined out on the story of his plane trip. Among the few friends he had in the city and at café tables where he got into conversation with other Americans, the story of the dying doctor who cried out *"Je suis le médecin"* never failed to get a big laugh. In the version that he told, however, David couldn't help but suggest that perhaps Dr. Mermelstein had somewhat exaggerated or invented his connections to Sartre, Camus, and Einstein. The story seemed to go better when Dr. Mermelstein was portrayed as a charlatan. In all tellings he described Inez as "like a character in a García Márquez novel," but only once, to two blond college students from Colorado, did he mention that he had desired her. By the time David returned to New York, having seen his book on three Parisian shelves but in no windows, he had forgotten Dr. Mermelstein's name and the story he told his Manhattan friends featured a "Dr. Melstein or something." Moreover, he no longer quoted *"Je suis le médecin"* but went straight for the translation "I'm the doctor." In New York, somehow it seemed less pretentious to avoid the French.

As for the Mermelsteins, they spent a pleasant week in Paris with Emanuel and Millie. Lothar felt no aftereffects from his unfortunate episode. As Inez was packing the trunk of their car to leave, Emanuel came to help her, and when she put down one of the heavy suitcases he squeezed her arm. The sensation that she felt was more or less equivalent to that which she had felt when he had touched her breast almost forty years earlier. For the first time, looking at this sixty-nine-year-old man, she wished that she had slept with him.

Lothar, as Inez had anticipated, drove extremely fast. Twenty kilometers from Madrid he spun their hired Citroen off a wet road and into a ditch. Inez spent the next week recovering from a broken collarbone and multiple contusions in a bed in the same hospital, La Paz, that Lothar's father had worked in after his arrival from Germany. Lothar was not so lucky. The steering column of the Citroen had penetrated his sternum, and after two desperate hours on the operating table, he died.

Lothar's obituary appeared two days later in the *New York Times,* accompanied by a photograph of the doctor taken on the day that he had been named chief of cardiology at Cedars-Sinai in 1962. Two half columns detailed the life and work. There was no mention of his "bacteria" theory, although his trip to Moscow received special attention on account of a small-scale international incident that had erupted at the airport when one of the other American doctors on the trip, Dr. Seymour, had been accused of trying to smuggle out three valuable icons. Lothar, the writer concluded, before listing the names of the bereaved, had been hotly tipped to win the year's Nobel Prize.

Several days later a nurse brought the paper to Inez. She read it without emotion. The Lothar she had known and loved could not be condensed in this way. How could she honor his memory? The answer, she thought, as the morning traffic in Madrid circled the hospital with its great democratic noise, was to live with passion. Immediately, she entertained the idea of returning to live in Paris, and by evening, shortly before she fell asleep, her mind was made up.

On the day that the obituary appeared, David, drinking coffee at home in his Manhattan apartment before setting off for work, had time to read the sports pages, the front page, and the first and last paragraphs of the Monday book review. He did not, however, reach the obit on page A21, where he would have learned, among other things, the names of Dr. Mermelstein's first two wives, one of which happened to be Mercedes.

Tosh

Tosh parked his car, edging it as far as possible into the shade thrown by a purple jacaranda. He was going to lock it, then remembered that the door jammed if he did. He crossed to the cooler side of the street and walked in the direction of the Hotel Borne. He was early for his meeting and thought he'd stop for a drink at the Benny Hill, but the pub looked depressingly empty when he passed so he turned into Bertorelli's instead. Two witchy ancients with peroxide beehives stood rinsing beer mugs behind the bar. Bert, his ridiculous white ten-gallon hat tipped back on his head, was adjusting microphones on the tiny stage. Tosh took a thousand-peseta note out of his wallet and slid it across the bar. No one picked it up, and the note lay soaking in the effluence of a leaking pitcher of sangria.

"All right, are you, Tosh?"

"I'm all right."

"Not done anything naughty recently?"

"Not a thing."

If the American woman showed up at the hotel, he would really be all right. Night on the town, lots of munchies at her expense, night in the sack, maybe palm her wallet at the end, or something better—who knew? Free trip to New York, behave himself for a couple months, figure out the next move.

Bert adjusted a last cable, plugged it in, and tested the mike by singing "Little Arrows."

"It's a bloody time warp in here," Tosh said.

"If you don't like it, go somewhere else. You've got the whole of Magaluf. No one's twisting your arm to come in here."

Tosh took a sip of his beer, then fake-spluttered a little.

"Can't you even chill the fucking beer? You are in Spain, you know. It's hot outside, or hadn't you noticed."

Bert came over and sat on the bar stool next to Tosh.

"Have you got something for me?"

"What are you talking about?"

"Don't be an idiot."

"Oh, *that*."

Tosh reached into his pocket and brought out a pack of Marlboros. Bert plucked the thousand-peseta note out of its puddle, held it up to drip-dry, then handed it back to Tosh.

"And some," Tosh said.

"I know."

Bert went behind the bar and opened the till. He took out five thousand pesetas and handed the money over to Tosh; then he flicked the Marlboro lid and glanced at the thin slab of hash he had acquired. The peroxides looked the other way.

Bert stared at a small coffee stain above the pocket on Tosh's cream shirt.

"Not exactly Mr. Big, are you?"

"No," Tosh replied. "I'm Mr. Small."

The faux-timbered walls of Bertorelli's were covered with blown-up photographs of Italy's greatest architectural and artistic treasures: the Colosseum, Venice by night, *David*.

"Answer me this," Tosh said. "If you're Italian, why do you only serve curry?"

"I'm not Italian. I'm Irish. Bertorelli: Bert O' Reilly. Get it?"

"Not too often these days."

"You should've stuck it out with Angela."

"She wasn't amenable."

"Can't say as I blame her."

Tosh thought for a moment of his house in London. The mantelpiece above the fireplace with all the Toby mugs he'd collected down the Portobello Road. Angela in the kitchen. He grabbed her around the waist from behind and planted a kiss on the back of her neck. She couldn't handle his being in the Scrubs, even though it was only a six-month stretch. "You're like a bloody

116

punch-drunk fighter. You won't stop till they knock you out. I'm sick of it; the children are sick of it. It's the nineties, not the bloody sixties. You're too old for this kind of caper. Give it a rest or get out."

Bert was back at the microphone, rehearsing "My Old Man's a Dustman."

"I'm off," Tosh shouted. "I've got to go and meet someone."

"Where?"

"In 1997. The Tardis is waiting for me outside."

"Fuck you."

"Now, now," Tosh said.

He went out into the blinding sun and walked under the nose of the dusty grounded yellow aircraft that Bert had opened as a discotheque, then closed after the air-conditioning failed one night and a German tourist collapsed and died. Mallorca was English and German. The locals hardly counted. It was like the war all over again—that's what his father had said when he came to visit. But the old geezer was obsessed.

Tosh walked toward Fred's Fish and Chips, where a group of young women with kids in strollers were having lunch. He thought he'd get a plate but then changed his mind. As he went past, one of the women said, "Don't know whether he's coming or going, do he?" and the other, the blonde, bent double, laughing. The babies' mouths were streaked with ketchup. Someone had left a dirty diaper on one of the tables.

No respect for nothing, Tosh thought.

He came into the lobby of the Borne. Eleven-thirty

in the morning and the bar was already jammed. Bunch of hooligans in from Birmingham. Show 'em a little sun and they rush indoors to get a beer. Then they all rush out and get sunburn.

"Tosh?"

He turned quickly. It was her.

"Oh, hello, Amanda," he said. "I'm a bit early."

"No, I was," she replied.

"All right, are you, love? Can I get you a drink?"

She looked toward the crowded, noisy bar.

"Get out of here, shall we?" said Tosh, reading her thoughts.

They wound up in a little bar next door to the BCM disco.

"Guess where I'm going tonight?" she asked.

"I wouldn't know where to begin."

"Deia."

"Arty-farty town."

"I met this lovely English poet on the beach at Es Trenc, and he invited me to a dinner party in Deia. He said I could bring a guest. I thought you might like to come."

"What, me?"

"Why not?"

"Here's the only poem I know: 'Roses are reddish / violets are bluish / If it wasn't for Jesus / we'd all be Jewish.'"

"I'm Jewish."

"No offense."

Tosh thought for a minute that he might have blown it, but then it seemed as if she still liked him. After all, he'd been a gentleman the other night, not pushing too far and all that—never does to go overboard when you've just pushed out of port.

"All right," he said, thinking he could make amends for the Jewish joke, "I'll come with you."

They had lunch in the bistro down near the beach. Americans were unbelievable. They hadn't a clue. What a pleasure. She didn't get it at all, had no idea if he was some wanker from Walthamstow or a member of the royal family. She paid for lunch—gone and left his bloody wallet back at his place, hadn't he?—and Tosh kept the receipt. Receipts were useful; he'd once given a whole bunch to some journalist over on expenses to do the Lager lout violence and the birds. Stupid fuck was so happy, he gave Tosh a bottle of Glenfiddich and a free subscription to his magazine, *Racing Cars and Tarts*. That's what it should have been called, anyway.

The other thing is, Americans like to tell you everything about themselves. Amanda was twenty-nine (going on thirty-five), she lived in Brooklyn, and— would you believe it?—she worked in a bloody bank. Although her métier was pottery. Or was it poetry? One of the two. Either way, she'd definitely said "métier." Tosh liked that. An English woman might think it, but she'd choke before bringing a frog word up in conversation with Tosh, wouldn't think he'd know what it meant.

"What do you do?" she'd asked Tosh the previous evening.

They were sitting in Abacinto's, down where the white goat wandered around and the management had spilled oranges all over the floor for effect. Bert should give that a go. Amanda'd had about three gin fizzes, and Tosh felt she was coming on a little inquisitive.

"Maritime law," he replied. "I'm a pirate. You'd better watch out. This island's full of villains."

He'd never spoken truer words.

But they got on all right, and why not? He was a big handsome fellah, even if half his teeth needed capping. The girls still liked him. And she was on holiday, lonely, looking for a bit of safe sex with a local. He wasn't that, safe or local, but he was the next best thing.

He told her to pick him up at nine in the bar at the Hotel Son Vida; dinner wouldn't be till at least ten and the drive was only forty minutes. They could go in his car, but unfortunately he'd promised to lend it to a friend, so it would have to be her rental.

Tosh drove back to his apartment in La Villetta. There were three messages on the answering machine. One from Angela about the bloody child support, and two from persons unknown interested in what he had to sell that might cheer them up for a few hours. Not tonight, my friends. Toshy had other fish to fry.

After a nap, a shower, and a little joint, he was ready. He put on his black jeans and his white shirt, then went up to the Son Vida. He hated them there. Last spring the management had allowed the police to tap a phone in the room of one of Tosh's overseas clients. Lost the deal and nearly had his whole little one-man operation busted open. Cost Tosh half his savings to keep the cops off his back.

Amanda appeared on the terrace in a white sleeveless dress. The foreigners always went señorita once they got a bit of a tan. Look at her. Great boobs and toned-up arms. That was another thing about American girls. They all exercised—looked like they were ready to wrestle, not fuck.

"Hello, darlin'," Tosh said, planting a kiss on her cheek and giving her a squeeze. "How about a quick one before we go?"

Amanda gave him a dirty look, but there was a smile at the end.

"No, no, don't get me wrong now—drinkies, sweetheart."

Preliminaries. Tosh enjoyed them. The chatting, being charming, all that stuff.

They sat outside. The terrace fell away into nothing. Beyond, the lights of Palma, a constellation of which suddenly seemed to levitate. A plane, of course, busiest airport in Europe or something like that. Quality stuff Tosh had gotten his hands on this time: Paki brew.

Chat, chat. A couple of Mancunians at the next table talking about the bloody glass factory they'd visited.

"I love it here," Amanda said. "I don't want to go back."

"That's what happened to me," Tosh replied. "I came over for a holiday, breathed in some of that sea air, took a quick look around, downed a couple of bottles of Chateau Cheapo, and thought, this is for me." *Thought they weren't going put you away for walking around with half an ounce, more likely.* Still, no need for the nasty details.

They drove up to Deia. Tosh took the wheel. Nice and slow around the terraces, no show-offy stuff.

"Lovely view by day." Tosh indicated the villages below with a jerk of his head. "Red rock."

Amanda fumbled in her straw shoulder bag. Tosh flicked on the car's interior light.

"Here's the address," she said. "I hope they remember inviting me."

The apartment was above an art gallery on the village's main street. A woman with cascading blond curls but a face a bit too old for her hairstyle was standing on the narrow balcony. When she saw Amanda and Tosh she yelled down, "Hey, hold on. I'll throw you the keys."

They entered through a wooden door, then climbed a spiral staircase, which opened into a small kitchen that itself led to a roof garden with an expansive view of the surrounding cliffs. As they stepped outside Amanda did one of those approving sharp intakes of breath, as if the air were full of jasmine. In fact, it was full of smoke of the type Tosh liked very much.

There were two women and a man sitting at a low, round table that featured a bowl of black olives and two bottles of wine. The poet, Mr. Skinny with a mop of curly hair out of 1968, was cooking something up in the kitchen.

"Amanda. Right? So glad you could come. And this is?"

"My friend Tosh. You did say."

"Oh, yeah. Glad to meet you. Michael Sutcliffe."

Skinny waved a spoon instead of shaking hands.

They were all English, Tosh reckoned, and it turned out he was right. James, Liz, Tina, one of the last names double-barreled. Gilbert-Fogg, something like that. Amanda lapped it all up.

Everything went fine for the first half hour. The usual crap. How long? Just for the summer? Oh all year-round? That sort of thing. Harmless bunch, common summer fare, straight from Islington. Magaluf and lager for the total wankers, Deia and wine for this lot. They were passing the J's and Tosh was feeling quite happy staring at the scenery. Then his fellow Brits got a bit bored and started in on Amanda for not smoking dope. It was always the same: set an American among them for long enough and they couldn't resist teasing. Jealousy, really, Tosh always thought.

"Not worried about our saliva, are you?"

"Do you belong to a health club?"

Fortunately, before Tosh had to punch someone, Skinny came out licking his wooden spoon.

"We're just about ready."

Halfway through the meal (a not-half-bad paella), drunk and stoned, Tosh let out that he'd done some time in Wormwood Scrubs. Everybody got excited. He wasn't so drunk that he didn't doctor the story a bit for Amanda. He was young, nineteen, peddling a little dope—well, all right, a lot of dope. We all make mistakes. Bloody judge, no mercy. Three months. They all started leaning forward around the dinner table as if this were the best night of their lives. A genuine convicted felon in their midst. A victim of the system. Tosh looked across at Amanda. The news seemed to be going down all right. She even gave him a little ankle rub under the table. Lovely.

Tosh caught James Quentin-Hogg or whatever his name was staring at Amanda's tits. Then the trouble started, because he was actually staring at the little silver Star of David that had worked free over the top of her dress. James got a glint in his eye.

"Not to change the subject," he said, staring at Amanda, "but have you read the latest from Palestine? It really is quite unbelievable what the Israelis think they can get away with."

Tosh put down his wineglass. He really didn't give a toss what went on in the Middle East, but he knew an act of personal provocation when he saw one. Then Skinny got in on the act.

"We had a West Bank poet visit last week. Terrible stories. And apparently there's this incredibly rich Miami Jew, a billionaire or something, who simply buys up land around Jerusalem and hands it over to fanatics."

"Four bloody acres," James added.

They were all smashed. One of the women, Blondie, looked a little embarrassed.

"Jewish," she whispered to Skinny. "Don't say 'Jew.'"

"A rich Miami Jewish? What on earth are you talking about? How can I say that?"

"Call a Jew a Jew, that's what I say." James took his napkin and wiped some rice from his face.

Amanda rose from her chair.

"Where's the bathroom?"

There were suppressed giggles around the table.

"The loo is downstairs and out at the back, but don't go too far or you'll bump into the neighbor's donkey."

"You bunch of fucks," Tosh said quietly when Amanda had left the room. He wasn't threatening, just letting them know.

The room went quiet. They did "What team d'you support, then?" for a few minutes. Amanda came back. She looked as if she'd been crying but Tosh may have imagined that. The only light came from two candles in the middle of the table.

Incredibly, James Fartface started right up again as soon as she sat down.

"I have to tell you that the bad news about this island is that the place is just crawling with Germans, but the good news is that there are hardly any Jews."

Tosh gave him one right in the face, caught him on

the nose with his ring and gave him a nice little gash. Skinny thought of trying something, then thought better of it. Instead he said, "You asked for that, James."

Tina clumped downstairs, then ran back up with a roll of toilet paper.

"Sorry," she said to Amanda. "He gets like that. Doesn't mean it."

"Then why does he say it?"

Tosh took Amanda's arm. He saw that because she had replied aggressively their sympathy for her had immediately evaporated.

"Let's go," he said.

In the car on the way back, Amanda was silent for about ten minutes. Bad atmosphere. Tosh thought the whole night was probably fucked—never mind stealing her bag, or his trip to America. Finally, she spoke:

"Thanks," she said, "but you didn't have to do that."

"He had it coming."

Tosh took one hand off the wheel and placed it on Amanda's thigh. His knuckles were grazed. She let his fingers slide up toward her crotch, then arrested them at the vital moment.

"We don't want to crash over the edge," she said.

Tosh began to laugh, shaking his head a little from side to side.

"What is it?"

"Front-wheel skid," he replied, still laughing.

"Exactly what we don't want."

"No, no. Front-wheel skid. That's what we used to say in my neighborhood. Cockney rhyming slang. You must have heard of that. The Yanks love it. Apples and pears / stairs; tit for tat / hat; toil and strife / wife."

"Front-wheel skid?"

"Yid!" Tosh yelled the answer. "No offense," he said, unable to control himself. But Amanda was laughing too.

"Let's stop here for a little splendor in the grass," Tosh suggested.

"How about your place?" Amanda replied.

Tosh never let anyone into his apartment if he could help it. Too much stuff around if anyone got inquisitive while he was in the bog or the shower. He had that nice shelf of books on maritime and Spanish law—well, nothing wrong with that, except that he kept his false passport in one of them. He should have had a safe or at least a locked drawer. He should have had a computer instead of address books and ledgers filled with client's names and balances. But Tosh was old-style and a little bit proud of it.

Still, there was no harm tonight. Amanda had had a rough time. Tosh was her knight in shining armor. He couldn't wait to get his leg over, and she couldn't wait to let him.

Tosh unlocked the high black gate that led into the courtyard of his building. He was singing to himself: *"Little arrers in my heart."*

"What's that?"

"Worst song ever written."

They were at it as soon as they stepped into the kitchen. A bit fumbly but not hopeless. She undid the buttons of his shirt. He tried to unzip Amanda's dress but it stuck halfway down her back. Tosh had to content himself with slipping his hand through the side and onto her breast. Very, very nice. Ding! End of round one. Tosh needed a slash. It was a long one. He flushed the toilet and came out cheerful.

"I'm in the bedroom," Amanda called.

Tosh thought he'd make an entrance. He removed his trousers, underpants, and socks. Not in bad shape, considering. His penis was happily erect.

Tosh pushed open the door to his bedroom. There were two men sitting on the edge of the bed. One had Tosh's collected written works on his lap, and the other was holding rather valuable merchandise that Tosh had flattened and hidden in a CD case.

"Oh, fuck," Tosh said.

"Fuck is right," said one of the cops. He had an American accent. The other guy looked Spanish.

Tosh looked wildly around the room.

"Fucking . . ." Tosh reached for the connecting word, but he wasn't quite sure what to put there. "Fucking Jews," he finally said. "Fucking Jews."

True
Love

We take the floor in a cloud of eau de cologne. My mother sings under her breath, *"This is my lucky day. This is the day that I will remember for all my life,"* but breaks off when the Ronnie Fox Trio strikes up the chords to "True Love." We waltz past a circle of loopy grins and sporadic hand claps. Johnny Fox croons, *"I give to you and you give to me trooo love, trooooooo luv."* My mother dances on tiptoe and stares over my shoulder, monitoring guests for offensive behavior. On our second circuit I see Dad slumped in a chair, as pale as the icing on the bar mitzvah cake. Very bad behavior indeed. He looks to be coughing uncontrollably, but I can't hear him. As "True Love" reaches its Oedipal climax, my mother touches her hand to her head and delicately coifs the brown waves sculpted hours earlier by

Jonathan Wilson

Neil of Davis Salon. She's about to reach Nirvana when Aunt Fanny blunders into the room. Fanny's in a rat-fur coat and holding a small blue and white suitcase. She looks as if she's been waiting on a platform somewhere east of the Rhine for twenty years and has only now learned that the war is over and it's safe to go home.

"Oh my God," my mother mouths at my father, doing a tango tilt so no one will notice what she's saying. "It's not even wrapped."

Is that blood on my father's shirt?

"I'm sorry, Mildred," my father manages to get out. "I can't hear you."

"Love furreeeever trooooooo." My mother joins in with the last line, plants a wet kiss on my cheek, holds me at arm's length, then smooths down my hair. Meanwhile, Dad's flat on the floor and Joe Green, a family friend but also a doctor, is kneeling over him, thumping at his chest and yelling for sugar cubes. Too late. The band has already segued into "Let's Twist Again" and the guests take a collective step back "to watch the children dance."

Fanny's first on the floor, swiveling her horrible knees, wobbling her wrinkled, freckled cleavage, and beckoning in partners from a fifteen-foot radius. I fight my way through to Dad. They've got his head leaning against the back of a chair. My mother's finally noticed what's going on. She's got an expression on her face that I can describe only as *extremely pissed off.* Is it possible that Dad is going to ruin the greatest day of her life by dying? Yes! He is!

"Do you remember when things were really hummin'..."

My Uncle George yells, "Someone shut that fucking band up!"

My mother says, "Do you have to use language like that?"

"I'm sorry, Mildred," Dad splutters.

Moments later, without adding a word, he expires.

At the funeral, Mum makes me wear Dad's coat and his trilby hat with the feather. I look ridiculous. The same people who were doing the twist when Dad died come back to our house after he's buried and eat food left over from the disrupted bar mitzvah reception. My mother's still going on about Aunt Fanny's suitcase.

"Can you believe it? She brings a *suitcase* to a bar mitzvah!" It's as if the shock of witnessing such an act of stupidity caused my father's heart attack.

Polly Taylor, one of my mother's friends, clucks me under the chin and asks me what I want to be when I grow up.

"A footballer," I reply.

"Not an office manager like your dad?"

"No," I say, "a footballer." I've never heard anyone say they want to be an office manager. It would be like saying I want to be a diabetic when I grow up, just like my dad.

After everyone has gone, my mother slaps me across the face.

"I heard what you said," she yells. "Why couldn't you say a lawyer, something professional?"

"Footballers are professional."

She raises her hand again but has second thoughts.

Later, my mother says, "How about a game of Scrabble? Take our minds off things."

We use the velvet drawstring tile bag that Dad made one time when he was in occupational therapy. I'm about to add ODOMIZE (76 points) to the trailing S at the bottom of my mother's TEAS when the phone rings. It's my girlfriend, Pat McNally. She's been away on the Isle of Wight for two weeks.

"Guess what?" she says. "My family's decided to emigrate to Australia."

"That's all right," I reply. "My dad died."

A month later I go to see Philip Sanders, our family doctor. His surgery is in one the roughest parts of the neighborhood. I sit in his waiting room and look fixedly at the floor because Trevor Peacock of the Chapter Road gang is on a chair right opposite me. After about two minutes Peacock asks, "Who are you fucking staring at?"

I keep checking the pattern in the lino and pretend I haven't heard. Peacock repeats his question.

A green buzzer goes off and the receptionist tells me to go through.

On the wall behind his desk, Dr. Sanders has a picture Dad painted. Dad gave it to him after one of the times he nearly died and Sanders came to visit him in the National Heart Hospital. It's three droopy chrysanthemums in a glass bowl. Dad was just a beginner in art.

"What's the problem?" he asks. Sanders has a nice round shiny face, glasses, and thin brown hair.

"My mother. She's driving me nuts."

I explain about the broken dishes, tears, hysterical outbursts, listening in on my telephone conversations.

Sanders hears me out, looks at a card in front of him, then says, "Any recurrence of conjunctivitis?"

"No, it all cleared up with that ointment."

"So there's nothing actually wrong with you."

"Well," I say, reaching for a phrase, "I suppose I'm feeling a bit mental."

"You'll be all right," Sanders replies.

I nod.

"Looks like you're just about taken care of." He gives me a warm smile. "Give my best to your mother. She's having a rough time. Not easy to lose a husband at her age."

He presses the button that sets off the green buzzer. I ask if he minds if I leave by the side door rather than through the waiting room.

My mother has a tea party for her sisters and their husbands. It's the first social event she's organized in six months. She buys bridge rolls and smoked salmon and bakes an apple cake. Uncle Phil and Aunt Eva are the first to arrive. Eva jumps smartly out of their 1959 Riley, crosses the street, and enters the house. Phil's getting something out of the glove compartment. He seems to be taking his time. After a minute or two there's loud knocking on the door.

"Go and let your Uncle Phillip in," my mother says.

"Be a dear, will you?" Eva adds.

I go and answer the door. Phil falls right in and collapses at my feet. He's dead. This is all getting to be a bit too much. They put a large white napkin that was going to line a basket for slices of apple cake over Phil's face. Aunt Eva starts sobbing. I go up to my room and stare out over the garden toward the railway tracks in the park. Then I go back down. Phil's where he was when I left him.

In short order the following people arrive at our house: the police, someone delivering flowers to the wrong address, the milkman, who gets paid on Saturday afternoons, a doctor, all my other uncles and aunts, and Rabbi Rabinovich. It appears that they turn up in the wrong order, because when Rabinovich enters our house my mother says, "He should have been here first." On the other hand, as my Uncle George points out, Rabinovich had to walk over because he couldn't violate the proscriptions against riding on the Sabbath.

"He could have set out earlier," my mother responds.

Uncle Phil gets buried right next to Dad, which is strange because he's not Dad's brother but my mother's sister's husband. It turns out, though, that the two families bought contiguous spots and the Burial Society made a small mistake. The wives were supposed to be on the inside, flanked by the husbands, but now it will have to be the other way around. I'm pleased Dad's next to Phil because I know they got on and liked chatting to each other. Mildred and Eva are a bit upset, of

course. When their time comes they're going to be separated by the men for eternity, which wasn't what they
had planned, because after a certain age, apparently,
you simply prefer female company, especially that of
close relatives.

When they lower the coffin Aunt Eva cries and so
do I because I liked Uncle Phil a lot. Uncle Phil and
Dad once took me on a day trip from Folkestone to Boulogne. On the channel crossing Dad took a photograph
of a ferryboat that passed us going the other way. Later
he pretended it was the boat we'd been on. No one
could figure out how Dad got the shot. We took a bus
out of Boulogne and wound up in some village where
Phil bought peaches and we all, me included, drank a
bottle of wine. I threw up on the boat coming back.

Mr. Jessel from the hardware store comes up behind
me, indicates the descending coffin with a nod of his
head, then winks and whispers in my ear.

"If you've got any messages for your dad, now's the
time to pass them on."

I step forward to shovel dirt in the grave and
mumble, "Mum's driving me crazy. We have commercial TV."

After this funeral my mother sits in the kitchen
in total darkness. She's found a packet of cigarettes in
my jacket pocket and says Dad must be turning in his
grave. When I ask if that's so he can talk to Uncle Phil
more easily she throws a wet rag in my face.

A fortnight passes. I come home late from school
because I've gone over to Harlesden to spend some time

with Noreen Prince, who's Jamaican. My mother's sitting in the car outside our house in a light blue polka-dot summer dress. She's had her hair done and her face is made up. She's not going anywhere and she hasn't been anywhere; she's just sitting there.

I see her as I'm hitting top speed on the curve of our street, running in the final of the Olympic two hundred meters. As I break the tape next to the car my mother rolls down the window and says, "I know where you've been."

I'm not surprised, because before leaving the house I told her where I was going.

Then she adds, "Don't even think about visiting your father's grave."

"All right," I reply, "I'll try not to think about it."

She leans forward as if she might actually turn the ignition and start the car, but then she simply slumps forward against the wheel.

I go into the house. Her "drives" usually last a couple of hours, and longer if no one comes by. Sometimes she waits three and a half hours for a neighbor to appear walking a dog or carrying groceries, and then she gets out of the car as if she's just been somewhere and "bumps into" them.

I start staring out the window at the beginning of June, and it seems that I'm still staring at the end of August.

No one dies the whole summer.

Fat
Twins

Wenty's behind the wheel of his rusty yellow Volvo doing about eighty on a rare stretch of straight near his house. We are going to die like Thelma and Louise, but at the last second he crunches down the gears, takes a curve, and launches our descent from the hills over Kingston. He turns the radio up loud and because it's carnival week and everything is upside-down, the DJ plays jump-up from Trinidad instead of local reggae. "Who let the dogs out? Who? Who?" Wenty joins in the chorus, then turns half around in his seat. He's enjoying himself so much, he almost lets go of the wheel.

"Do you know who the dogs are, my friend?"

Alex shakes his head, then stares sullenly out the window; his arm rests on the glass as if he wants to punch through. Leyton, sitting next to him, just smiles.

"Men! Men like your father and me. Randy old men. Rabid, hungry, desperate."

Alex refuses to laugh.

"Only kidding," Wenty says. "We're pussycats."

The sinking sun spreads its last light over the brown horizon, and under it the precincts of the poor: wood and scrap-iron shacks, tin roofs and hasty signs (YES NOW OPEN FOR BUSINE THANG YOU FOR YOUR PATRONAGE HAVE NICE DAY'S), pigs, goats, and starving mongrel dogs.

By the time we hit the vicinity of the Bob Marley Museum, Wenty's drunk half the six-pack of Red Stripe that he jammed between the front seats before we set out. The air-conditioning coughs, buzzes, and pines, but the car is a furnace. Wenty doesn't seem to notice. A burned-spice scent of pork jerk penetrates the windows of the Volvo.

We pull sharply off the road in front of two boys on yellow BMX bicycles, almost knocking them off.

"Watch where you're going!" Wenty yells.

We make it for the last tour of the day.

In front of us in line are Christina and Jules, two tall, skinny, heels-hot-pants-and-cutoff-halter-top Louisiana working girls. They are out in Jamaica on a vacation swap: Fat Tuesday and the excess of New Orleans for Appleton rum and the winin' up of Jouvert. How do I know so much about them? Because Wenty's been chatting since we got out of the car.

"How come your pants so long?" he began, followed by, "I told myself the first woman I saw after the sun started going down I'd ask her to marry me. But I saw both of you at the same time. Now which of you ladies . . . ?"

Leyton's seen and heard his father's routines before, so he's acting cool and indifferent, but Alex is a study in concentration: the heat, the sculpted asses of the women, the funky wood figure of Bob Marley in his green and yellow fluorescent hat.

"This statue here shows Bob with his three favorite items: his gui-tar, his soccer ball, and his spliff."

Alex is all attention.

"Better than the Science Museum?" I murmur.

He scrunches up his face as if he's thinking about it. Then, for what seems like the first time in months, he smiles.

Am I a good dad or what?

Our guide looks like a schoolgirl, and it turns out that she is one, working the museum on a spring break job. Her name is Velma; she's very serious and won't respond to Wenty's questions. "Where you live, Velma? What's the name of your English teacher?"

We follow her past "Bob's herb garden," medicinal spliff-weed in abundance, and out around the back of the house, where a late-career Rasta lounges in a cracked wicker chair. His hands are cupped and he's sending smoke signals.

"And this gentleman you see here"—our guide stretches out her thin, schoolgirl arm and points—"is the famous Georgie who lit the fire light in Mr. Bob Marley's unforgettable song 'No Woman No Cry.'"

"No shit," says Christina.

"Yeah man," replies our guide.

Georgie doesn't register our presence. He carries on doing what he does best.

We see the bullet holes in the wall of the small kitchen where Bob got shot and a room wallpapered with yellowed newspaper clippings that document his success. We view the sparsely furnished master bedroom: an oil portrait of Haile Selassie on the wall, a dark varnished acoustic guitar on its stand at the foot of the bed. Jules and Christina bend over the rope that inhibits entry. Wenty sighs much too loudly. When the girls turn around and fake indignance, he pretends a mind elsewhere and says "Poor Bob."

I've known Wenty for thirty-five years, and I haven't seen him for twenty-five. When we met we were skinny boys smoking on a back street outside school. We were younger then than our sons are now. It seems impossible. On the edge of sleep last night, Alex said to me, "Wenty's just like you, Dad, only . . ."

"Only what?" I replied in a whisper, filling "you're divorced" in the guilty box at the front of my head. But Alex was out fast, the fan oscillating at the foot of his bed and music from a fete halfway down the hill curling up through the banana plants and star apple trees on the terrace outside.

We do the souvenir shop—Reggae Boys soccer T-shirt and a Bob-with-huge-joint bumper sticker for Alex's wall at home—then we go in for the video.

Alex says, "At home the shop's always at the end of the tour, never in the middle."

Fat Twins

Somewhere along the way we've lost Christina and Jules—and Wenty.

The film's grainy and the music echoing down the room has the same rough quality. When Bob starts "Don't Worry 'Bout a Thing" I recall Wenty wearing the track out on the night his father died. He must have lifted and dropped the arm of the record player more than twenty times. Beyond the windows of the Powells' front room the tube rumbled into Kilburn Station and showered yellow sparks over the railway bridge.

When we come out into the dusk, we spot Wenty over by the statue. He's got a girl on each arm and Velma's taking a group picture using Wenty's camera. Christina and Jules are each a head taller than Wenty, and his belly puffs out dropsically (*Wenty's just like you, Dad* . . .) like a speed bump between the exposed flatness of the girls' stomachs.

"Come on over here!" he shouts when he sees us. He pushes Alex and Leyton into the space that he's vacated between Christina and Jules.

"Go ahead, Velma, take the picture. Smile, Alex, smile. You can show this to your friends at home. What Jamaica did for you. But don't show your mother."

Don't show your mother.

"You're taking him where?"

"To Jamaica."

"Are you crazy? Nobody goes to Jamaica anymore. It's dangerous."

"I promised if he got on the honor roll."

"But he didn't! He got two C's and a D!"

"It was too late. I'd already made the booking."

"And the dope?"

"I'll make sure he stays out of trouble."

"He's a Phish-head."

"I know."

"Do you *remember* that he was suspended from school last year?"

"He was having a tough time."

"We were all having a tough time—except you. Now you're simply trying to ingratiate yourself after what you did."

"I didn't do anything."

"You broke up a family."

"I thought you agreed with Dr. Sloane that the responsibility for our failures was mutual."

"Why not Florida? If he *has* to go somewhere for spring vacation. He could stay with my parents in Boca."

"But Wenty invited . . ."

"Who's Wenty?"

"He's an old friend. Wenty Powell."

"An old friend you haven't mentioned in twenty years."

"That's not true."

It is true.

"Well who is he, anyway? Is he . . . involved?"

"Jesus Christ. He's not a drug dealer and he's not a Rasta. Wenty's got a kid Lexie's age and happens to be in the bloody government. I don't think we can be in much safer or more responsible hands."

*His father was in the government, but not Wenty.
Wenty runs a Volvo dealership.*

"Why should a man your age need to be 'in safe hands'?"

"I was only trying to reassure you."

"Where does this Wenty live?"

"In Kingston."

"Are you nuts? They rob and kill white people in Kingston."

"That's racist propaganda."

"Oh, God, I hate you. Alex can't go. He can't."

"He wants to."

"Well, he's not going."

"I told you, I've already bought the tickets."

Tonight's party (O happy country!) is at the home of a junior trade official with whom Wenty once worked in Trinidad. You have to be invited and then you have to pay for your ticket. It's a low white house not too far down the hill from Wenty's place. We drive, Wenty and Hera in the front seats, the rest of us in the back.

Wenty behaves himself when Hera's around; or, rather, he performs an exaggerated version of the good husband: courteous, controlled, considerate, affectionate. I'm jealous of his successful performance, although when Hera, tall and imperious, widens her almond-shaped eyes, she seems to scan right through Wenty's pressed shirt and into his wild Jamaican heart. Hera's high class from St. Martin's—smart, churchgoing, a serious money manager for a large corporation. A rascal like Wenty is lucky to have found her. On the other hand, Wenty is full of love. He's got so much that it overflows from the seams of his being and comes out as flirtatious talk. So what? Neither Hera nor anyone else on the island is going to impeach him for that.

Out back of the house the DJ's high on a scaffolded platform and the garden's a thick bubble of grace and funk under hot stars. The song in progress concerns a plumber who uses his tool to get a female client's water flowing. All over the lawn the dogs are out barking up the wrong trees. There are kids dancing and grannies too, and everybody in between locomoting around.

"Katrina," Wenty calls, "dance with this young man—he afraid of the Jamaican girls. They too forward, shovin' their behinds at him, so he getting all confused and upset."

"I'm not upset," Alex says. He's got a tumbler of rum and Coke in his right hand, or maybe it's only Coke. How should I know? Wenty starts to dance with Katrina himself and shouts over her shoulder.

"She comes here every year from Oslo, just for Jouvert. She like the jump-up music."

There are five more hours until dawn, when semi-naked mud-smeared women will roam the carnival streets in search of a likely man or adolescent boy to press themselves against. "In America," Wenty asked Alex, "you have to pay women to do that, right?"

Wenty's sister Lucy steps up behind me, grabs my arms, and starts them in motion. She's like a swim instructor demonstrating a new stroke, but in a way that's likely to bring on a harassment suit. Someone passes around a yard glass of vodka, and then a yard of rum punch. The dogs are baying at the low Caribbean moon. Hours pass before I notice Alex is gone.

We look first in the dark corners of the garden where no food or drinks are being served; then we pass inside the house. Alex isn't there and the guards posted at the front and rear doorways haven't seen a white boy with a blond ponytail strut by or through. We are about to venture into the street when Wenty's friend Rex comes up with the news that someone saw Alex and Katrina leaving in a taxi.

"Oh, well he's OK, then," Wenty says, half turning back to the garden and ready to party on.

"What do you mean?"

"She's a very responsible young lady. And she's staying over with Lorna Greene down near Redbones bar. There's probably a fete there. Your son is in good hands, man. And with any luck her little Norwegian titties are in his hands."

"But I have to find him."

"No, man. Let him be. It's carnival. Leyton'll go over for a report."

"I'll go with him."

"You stay here. Listen to the music. Loosen up a

little more. You have a life ahead of you. You're not a happily married man like myself. There's a woman I want you to meet, Nicola, recently without a man on account of his moving to New York to found a chapter of the Ethiopian Zion Coptic Church, if you know what I mean."

"I don't."

Wenty puts his thumb and forefinger to his lips and delivers two sharp intakes of breath.

"Hey, Leyton," I shout. He is already opening the door of a friend's car. "Wait for me."

Wenty shakes his head.

"Taken his driving test and failed three times. The examiner waiting for me to bribe him. No way I'm gonna do that, man. People in this country got to learn to behave the proper way. This kind of petty stuff. Harassin' tourists, that kind of thing. That's not how you get an economy moving."

Leyton gets out and lets me in the back seat. Two teenage Chinese girls in leather miniskirts squeeze over.

"Make more room for Uncle Timmy," Leyton gently orders them.

There is no more room to make.

We speed through four-way intersections and red lights with only the briefest pauses, as if there were brigands instead of churches on every corner.

At Redbones the parking lot is jammed full, so Leyton's friend drops us by an archway entrance to the garden. The scent of jasmine fills the night air. There's a soca band set up at the far end of the lawn, and as we arrive they announce a fifteen-minute break.

"I'll go find Lorna Greene," Leyton says.

I search the crowd for Alex and Katrina's blond heads. When I find them they turn out to belong to Jurgen and Elena, a middle-aged couple from Tübingen in Germany.

It must be a half an hour before Leyton returns in the company of Lorna Greene, a skinny, high-cheek-boned woman who is wearing a skintight red sheath.

"A woman always looks good in a red dress." Wentworth Powell.

"Timmy Milton," she says. "Wenty told me all about you. Underage drinking in London. Rugby songs. Two naughty boys. You know my first husband, Len Greene, went to the same school as you and Wenty—but he was two years younger."

She kisses me on the cheek. If Alex wasn't lost my heart would burst open, pulpy and orange like a split mango.

"I'm sorry, but your son has left, although I don't think he's sorry." Lorna offers a wide smile.

"What do you mean? Where is he?"

"They've gone to Jouvert in Negril. Katrina's got a rental car, and she offered to take him down. There's always a whole crowd there. They dive off the rocks at dawn."

They crack their heads open. The few who surface are taken to hospitals.

"I can't believe he didn't . . ."

"Oh, I promised him I'd explain when you came looking. Katrina said they'd be back the day after tomorrow."

The night is very dark and I am standing at the bubbling confluence of two black rivers, love and anger.

"How long is the drive to Negril?"

"That depends. Three, four hours."

"Oh, Jesus."

Leyton turns toward a table near the bar where the girls he brought with him have settled down next to two handsome dudes in their twenties.

"Leyton, can you please take me back to your father?"

Prig.

"Sure, Uncle Timmy," he says, although I can tell that he doesn't want to make the journey.

"I'll drive you," says Lorna Greene.

We are in a midnight blue Volvo speeding through the midnight blue night—Wenty appears to have sold a car to almost every friend that he has on the island. The hem of Ms. Greene's dress kisses the horizon of her narrow thighs. The radio is on, of course, and Lorna sings along. There's a tiny silver crucifix at her throat, settled in the glowing cavity that the English Patient wanted to know the name of.

"Now, how long have you been divorced?" she asks.

"Six months."

"After?"

"Seventeen years."

"What happened?"

"We had an argument about wallpaper, then Mara didn't want to get a dog, then a couple moved in next door who seemed more happily married than we were, and it all went downhill from there."

"But things started well?"

"Don't they always?"

"Did you cheat?"

"I did not have sexual relations with that woman."

"And how is your son taking it?"

"Not well. As you see."

"He might have run off anyway. Wouldn't you? If you were sixteen and with Katrina?"

"I wouldn't have had the guts."

Lorna laughs, and I get a trembling in my belly like a guava jelly. Or maybe that's just the words of the song coming out of the radio.

It's when I ask Wenty to lend me his car that he decides to drive me.

"No," I continue. "I don't want you to miss Jouvert."

"I've seen plenty of Jouverts in Kingston, man. And anyway, Hera asked me home by five because she's going out early to visit her sister in Port Antonio and you're giving me a good excuse not to be there. But wait, let's load up first."

We have two bottles of Appletons, a liter of ginger

ale, a bag of ice, and a six-pack of Red Stripe. Somewhere, halfway between Kingston and Negril and not far
from a crude wooden sign that designates the birthplace
of the murdered reggae star Peter Tosh, we will stop to
buy shrimp from barefoot women with overflowing bas-
kets who rush the roadside when we slow down. But by
then I will be in a semi-stupor brought on by alcohol
and the dark clots of irresponsibility inside my brain.

"At Mandeville, I have to pop in on my auntie and
pick something up," Wenty says.

"Is this a real relative or someone like me?"

"No, man, this my mother's younger sister."

My stomach leaps as the road curves, seemingly
forever.

"This is the longest bend in Jamaica. Strange,
isn't it?"

"How could you possibly know that?"

"There's one highway, man, and there's one bend
like this."

The old Volvo climbs toward Auntie's house. Beneath us the earth slashed red by bauxite mining shows
purple in the moonlight. We pass an old stone church,
turn up to the peak of a hill, then swing into a long
driveway. At Auntie's house the front rooms are dark.

"You stay here," Wenty says. "Your eyes are red. You
look like you need to close them. Take a nap. I'll be
right back."

I watch him weave toward the front door. Wenty's
large head lolls slightly to the right and his silver
dollar–size bald spot recedes to a spot of light.

Wenty rings the bell and waits. Over his shoulder the sky brightens behind the ackee and almond trees. A hummingbird flashes its iridescent green breast across the garden. I reach for a beer but we have already dispatched the six-pack. Time to move on to the rum.

"Auntie must be away," he shouts. "I'm going to try the back door. Hera left her hair dryer last time we visited."

I remain in the front seat of the car for about five minutes, and then I start thinking about Alex and how my dream of bonding and forgiveness has turned into a nightmare of separation and rejection. What did I expect?

I get out of the car.

At the side of the house there is a shiny new Volvo station wagon parked beside a small white garage, and beyond that the land falls sharply away.

They dive off the rocks.

Away to my left, I see Wenty at the back door, jiggling with the lock. He doesn't hear me as I approach, and I can hear him mumbling.

"Can't believe it. She's had the bloody locks changed. Shit, oh fucking shit."

"Hey," I say, "what's going on?"

Wenty starts back.

I peer through the window of the back door. A light that must have burned all night serves up a surprise: aqua blue walls and what appear to be a set of framed erotic black-and-white photographs.

"Let's go," Wenty says, and grabs my arm.

151

"This isn't your aunt's house, is it?"

"It certainly is. Auntie! Auntie!" Wenty moves forward and raps on the window with his knuckles.

"Give me a break."

"Auntie! Auntie! Are you in there?"

At this moment, as there is no privacy in the nutshell world, Wenty's cell phone rings, but because there is no justice in the world either and because technology has plugged an outlet for paranoia into the satellite-dusted skies, the person on the other end is my ex-wife and not Hera.

"Where is he?" she says, her voice as clear and honest as a cowbell. "Where is Alex? I just spoke to Hera Powell and I heard a definite catch in her voice when she gave me this number."

"A catch?"

"Put him on."

"He's not here. He's with Leyton, Wenty's son. They're in the car ahead of us. We're all going to Negril."

"Who's *driving* the car ahead of you?"

"Leyton."

"I thought you said he was sixteen."

"Eighteen. No, nineteen, almost twenty."

"I can't *believe* you let him drive with another boy."

"Oh, believe me, Leyton's a better driver than . . . I can't hear you. The line's all fuzzy. I'll call you from the hotel."

I press the power button. Wenty has slumped to the ground and is leaning his large back against the door.

The air is cool, but we're both panting heavily, as if we've taken Heart Attack Corner at high speed.

"Tell me who lives here!" I yell, in order not to be angry with myself and, through redirected rage, to prevent my son from plunging to his death.

"Vivette."

"Not your Aunt Vivette."

"No."

"And Vivette has changed the locks on the happily married man."

"That appears to be the case."

"Jesus, my teenage son has run away and is about to swan dive into oblivion, and you take a break just so you can fuck someone!"

"Bullshit! Don't be so fucking self-righteous. You always were, and anyway your son is about to live a little!"

Back in the car I weaken from anger to anxiety to misery. Wenty takes a swig of the Appletons, then hands the bottle to me. As if to cheer himself up, he announces, "I fucked your girlfriend, that Angela, when you went up to Leeds one weekend in the winter of 1968."

"I know," I murmur.

"Oh, you know."

"She told me. She felt very guilty. Don't worry. I forgave you both in the mid-1980s."

"I also fucked her for six months after that on

Sunday mornings when you thought she was going to St. Mary's Church with her mother. Then she got acne in that apartment on Kilburn High Road. Her face broke out something awful. Terrible pimples."

"That I didn't know."

"About the pimples?"

"No, about the serial fucking."

"Oh, yes, we had a lovely time."

Away to our left, where Wenty is pointing, the sun has broken behind the frame of a large house set in spacious, empty fields.

"Big House, now it's a museum. She was a beautiful girl, Angela."

"Before the pimples."

"Yes. Here, I dug this up for you."

One hand on the wheel, Wenty reaches into his back pocket, extracts his wallet, flips it open, and removes a dog-eared photograph. He holds it gingerly for a moment between his thick fingers, then passes the picture over.

"No pimples on the body," I say.

"No," he replies. "None at all."

Wenty turns on the radio.

On the terrace of Rick's Café a multitude of spring break kids, mostly buffed-up male Americans, has gathered to cheer and watch the divers and jumpers swallow, fall, or plummet sixty feet into surging black water. The board is a thin outcrop of rock where each figure stands alone for a moment and then is gone. At the mouth of the bay a white catamaran from the Sandals Hotel launches a shoal of snorklers into rippling waves.

We make our way past abandoned breakfast tables, through the bands of higglers selling T-shirts, and out to the edge of the crowd. A deep collective sigh starts deep and pitches high because not one but two slim bodies have stepped to the narrow ledge. One of them belongs to my pink-chested son. On one leg each, like flamingos, Alex and Katrina, joined at the hip, hold hands and, stretching out their free arms and legs, construct a star that freezes for a moment then twists grotesquely out of shape as they fall and free-fall like the last weeks, months, or years of a bad marriage.

"Beautiful," Wenty says. "A lovely, brave jump."

"Where are the fat twins?" Leyton asks.

"In there," Hera replies.

Wenty and I pretend that we have not heard.

We watch the news beamed from Miami. After a while Wenty gets up and says good night. He pads slowly into his bedroom. Alex lies on the wood floor, reading the back of a CD.

"Listen," I say, "the first night we were here, you said I was just like Wenty only . . . and then you fell asleep. Only what? I'd like to know."

"Only?" Alex rolls over on his back and stares up at the ceiling.

"Well, what?"

Jonathan Wilson

The fan turns its unforgiving face back and forth between us.

"Only your bald spot is bigger than his. That's what."

"Oh," I reply. "I thought you were going to say something else."

Last
Light

I was back in Dublin after twenty years. My cousin Eve was dying in a small room above an antique shop down on the quays. She had been suffering from pancreatic cancer for eighteen months and now she was close to the end. In the mornings I left the smoke-filled foyer of the Shelbourne Hotel and walked down Grafton Street then around the back of the National Bank. I breakfasted alone at the Elephant in the renovated area on the south bank of the Liffey where, in the last few years, trendy cafés, galleries, and clothing stores had bloomed in the radiant colors of spring to replace the gray pubs and brown cobbled streets of my early childhood. Around ten I would cross the narrow footbridge over the river and visit my cousin.

Eve and I were the same age, fifty-five. Our mothers were sisters. My family had left for England when I was twelve while hers had remained in Dublin. We were both only children, uncommon creatures in this city of loose, sprawling families, and doubly strange because we were Jews. On Saturday mornings, after synagogue, we played diabolo—"the devil on two sticks"—on the roof of Eve's father's furniture shop on Lombard Street. At the end of her turn Eve would send the wooden cone flying above the chimney pot and accomplish a deft catch on its string when it fell. She had a lovely sense of balance.

Our parents were dead, and Eve's own children were grown and spread around the globe: a son in Israel, a daughter in Canada, another daughter in Australia. In a few weeks they would all be here to kiss their mother good-bye. Eve's ex-husband, Bernie Soams (they'd had to move to Manchester for a year to get the divorce), had disappeared down the deep well of America years ago after one of his liquid adventures in the stock market had turned to stone.

"Look at that," my cousin said. She was sitting up in bed reading the *Irish Times;* her morphine tablets sat like an hourglass next to a tumbler of water on her bedside table. "There they go, blaming the Jews. Can you believe it, Harry? After all these years of good behavior."

"Ours or theirs?" I replied.

"Why, theirs, of course. Do you think I'm a self-hater?"

She folded the paper and pushed it toward me over the blue counterpane.

I read the front-page article: a right-wing nationalist party, Muintir na hEireann, had publicly vilified two Jewish parliamentarians for pushing a yes vote in the divorce referendum. What, the group's leaders wanted to know, did the Jews know about Irish marriage? An aging judge and a country priest in his dotage had endorsed the sentiment.

"*Irish,* Harry. Do you see that? As if it were synonymous with *Catholic.*"

"It almost is," I replied.

"And what about the Travelers? The Protestants? The TD for County Clare is an Asian fellow. There's more Moslems here now than there are Jews."

"That isn't hard."

"So you say. Sad, sad. We're a vanishing people. Everybody knows it. What is it, Harry, nine hundred left in the city? Eight hundred? And you can be sure that's an exaggeration."

It had begun to rain, a soft drizzle that misted the windows of my cousin's room. Her big walnut bed had once belonged to her mother, my Auntie Mary: she had brought it in pieces on the boat from Lithuania and had it reassembled in Cork before forwarding it on the back of a cart to Dublin. "How did the Jews get to Ireland?" Mary used to ask. "The boat pulled up in Cork in the middle of the night, someone shouted 'New York!', and all the stupids got off."

"A bit rainy to walk today," I said.

"A little stroll, Harry, that's all. I need the air. Then I'll be tired and you'll be free of your duties to the sick."

We took our slow, familiar path back across the river and toward St. Stephen's Green. Once there my cousin needed to rest, so we sat on a bench and watched two elegant swans glide upon the water. The trees were coming into leaf, a small press of renewal that in the chill and silvery morning seemed like a false promise.

"Would you do a thing with me?" my cousin asked. "There's somewhere I want to go tomorrow."

"The old neighborhood again?" I replied. "You're incorrigible."

Making Eve laugh was like opening a music box; she had the same melodic register she'd had as a child.

"No," she said, "worse. I want you to take me to Friday night services."

"Now, what's brought this on?"

"I don't know. An expectancy, something, a hope."

We had, both of us, abandoned organized religion in our teens. I had gone on to commit the cardinal sin by marrying out of the faith. Eve certainly hadn't been among those who'd cared. Her local synagogue on Adeleide Road, she'd once told me, held nothing for her but a memory of endless tedium. The high nostalgia to which I sometimes succumbed for the old brick building permeated by Hebrew chant and packed with swaying men in prayer shawls, peppermint breath on Yom Kippur, the rabbi in his white robes and white plimsolls, the women in fur stoles, the swirl of autumn leaves when we exited—all this was stuff and nonsense to my cousin. Nevertheless, the thought of an Ireland without Jews was anathema to her.

"It's a special thing," she said. "We were a lovely community. All from Lithuania. No Poles. Good-natured, good people. Irish friendliness and a Jewish *kopf*. Is there a greater model for a human being, Harry, than Leopold Bloom?"

"The Blooms?" I said. "Now didn't they live in Rathgar and the daughter Sandra get pregnant by her violin teacher?"

My cousin pushed my arm, but it was a light touch, the strength ebbing out of her even as she tried to stem the pain brought on by sudden movement.

"Are you sure you want to go to *shul*, Eve?" I continued.

"I feel compelled in that direction, yes. Now escort me home before this rain swells and soaks us through."

On Friday by late afternoon the lobby and adjoining ground-floor bars in the Shelbourne were jammed with Welshmen in for the next day's rugby international. I wriggled into the boozy crowd, pushing a lane through dark suits, each lapel brightened by a daffodil. *"Bread of heaven,"* the Welshmen sang, *"feed me till I want no more."* At the bar I downed a double scotch, and then I was out in a crush of pedestrians all hurrying under a pale green plume of cloud past the city's brightly lit shops.

I had more than an hour before sunset, when the service to usher in the Sabbath would begin, so instead of going straight to Eve's I lingered around Trinity, browsing books and the occasional clothing store. Wherever I stood my eyes strayed in what was, for me, a local direction—toward the building's doorknobs. We, that is, our family on both sides of the Irish Sea, have been in the doorknob business since 1906, when my grandfather Shmuel brought his molds with him from Kaunas and set up a small workshop in Cork. The Levinsons are an unadventurous lot, which is why our branch of the tribe never made it to New York, and we have stuck, or been stuck, with the business through four generations.

In order to appreciate doorknobs you must first think about how people enter and leave a room. The doorknob is both handle and key and demands a turn of the wrist that helps us curb our natural pushiness on the way in. "Slow down," the doorknob says. "You are entering a private domain." In the other direction it gives us something to hold on to in those sometimes awkward moments of departure. Moreover, as my father used to remind me, door hardware is often the only tactile interaction we have with a building, our intimate connection to domestic and commercial structures. He also used to say "Ingress will be our egress," meaning that the doorknob—cast, chased, engraved, plated, and gilded—would help us rise above the ranks of the middle class and into the world of the truly rich and blessed. We have done all right, but I am not a wealthy man.

I wandered into Brown Thomas (where the knobs, I noted, were highly ornate), thinking that I might find a small gift for Eve, a silk scarf perhaps, for her to wear on our synagogue excursion. Eve's hair had thinned during her chemotherapy. On the first floor a sign rested on a gilt easel: AT FOUR PM IN THE LINGERIE DEPARTMENT MEET STUART KLINE AS LEOPOLD BLOOM. Both names were familiar to me. I followed the arrow into an open space next to the bra counter. There, in a bowler hat and dark three-piece suit, was my old school friend Stewie Kline. He was fingering a sheer slip with one hand and holding a copy of *Ulysses* in the other. A large group of shoppers, mainly women, formed a semicircle around him while he read some dirty but not too dirty bits from the great novel. At the end, Stewie plugged a line of underwear, which checked the laughter he had generated and arrested the applause that had begun in appreciation of his act.

"Is this a living Stuart?" I asked, approaching the speaker when the crowd had drifted away.

Mr. Bloom looked at me for a moment before a smile crossed his face.

"Mother, I didn't recognize you," he said, and then added, "Are you buying undies for a secret lover, Harry?"

We went out in search of the nearest pub, Stewie still in his costume. He gathered a few looks but fewer than one might imagine. The new European Dublin is sophisticated; like Amsterdam or Paris the streets accommodate numerous theatrical dressers and a properly blasé audience to observe them.

We sat in the snug of the Bleeding Horse. I told Stewie about Eve, but he knew, of course. The whiskey we were drinking burned in my throat.

"Can you believe this fucking job I've got?" said Stewie, and he started to laugh. "They send me all over the fucking world. I've sold nighties in Australia. This is what it's come to, Harry."

"Everybody has to make a living," I replied. "And if Leopold Bloom is helping you in that direction, I'm sure Mr. Joyce wouldn't mind. I believe he was fond of money."

"I wanted to be an actor."

"I remember."

"And I became a pitchman."

The barmaid came and stoked up the fire in the snug. It flamed briefly, then settled to an orange glow.

"And once upon a time I went out with your cousin. She was too clever for me."

Stewie had placed his bowler on the table next to our drinks. Now he picked it up and dusted off the rim.

"I'll tell you the truth, Harry, I don't give a fuck about the Jews. If the community dies it's their own fucking fault. If the Jews disappeared from New York or from Israel, now that would be serious. But from here? You're dealing with fucking headbangers. Parochial shit."

We had another round of drinks. Stewie lit a cigarette.

"Did Bloom smoke?" I asked.

"Who the fuck cares? He wasn't even a proper Jew. It was his father who was the Jew. It's perfect, isn't it. Suits the Irish sense of humor to celebrate a Jew that never existed, and he wasn't a Jew anyway."

A scrum of rowdy Welshmen, one draped in his country's flag, the others with daffodils in their caps, burst through the door; two burly barmen went to cut them off.

"Not in here, gentlemen. This is a quiet pub tonight."

It was time to go and fetch Eve. I bought Stewie a parting drink, had a quick double myself, then left him in the snug. The sky, waiting for the sun's pale fire to abandon it, had turned a dusky neutral gray. I felt light-headed from the whiskey and passed through Temple Bar in a daze, jostled by shop workers heading home or into the pubs and cafés. The Liffey had lost its usual dirty green and looked treacherously cold and steely. I imagined the River Neman flowing through Kaunas, with Grandfather on the bank following its icy passage. For a moment the whole of Dublin seemed to show a Baltic face. I touched my head as if a fur hat might have sprouted there.

I rang Eve's bell to warn her that I was on the way up. She was in the habit of leaving the door to her flat slightly ajar: it was a burden for her to rise from bed for visitors. I expected Eve to be dressed and ready, but there was no one at home. In her overheated bedroom the blue counterpane was rolled back and the sheets

165

disturbed. Eve's morphine was gone from her bedside table and her nightdress lay crumpled on the floor. Should I call the hospital? No need for panic yet. Surely she wouldn't have gotten dressed if she were in an emergency. I looked at my watch. Perhaps I had lingered overlong in the pub, downed one too many whiskeys, lost track of the time. I still felt unsteady in a slightly pleasant way. I walked to the window and looked out. The owner of the Castle Watch company next door was locking the yellow door to his offices. I tapped on Eve's window, then pushed it open.

"Mo, have you seen my cousin?"

"About an hour ago. I was in to Nick Miller's and she passed me on Halfpenny Bridge."

"An hour? Was she all dressed up?"

"I couldn't tell you, Harry. A black hat, maybe."

I went down onto Ormand Quay and walked fast toward the corner of O'Connell, where I thought I might pick up a taxi. The streets were busy and traffic stalled, so I crossed the bridge and headed south. Then I saw Eve in her midnight blue coat hurrying fifty yards ahead of me. I called out to her to stop, but a honking of horns drowned me out, then those damn Welshmen were in my way, spilling in and out of pubs and between cars, singing, cavorting: how they loved their nation.

I caught up with Eve halfway down Grafton Street when she stopped to peruse a flower stall, but of course it wasn't her. The woman I had been following was at least thirty years younger than my cousin; the hair tucked under her black felt hat was thick and dark brown, her skin unwrinkled. I apologized, but when she continued on her way I found myself trailing behind her. True, she was headed in my direction, but what was my direction? I had intended to catch up with Eve at the Adeleide Road synagogue, but I was drunk and open, more or less, to any course. And so I followed my blue-coated marker as she took a circulatory amble around the green and onto somber streets where my early childhood was stored like a forgotten toy in the shadowy corner of a dark cupboard. We passed Ehrlich's, the kosher butcher, and farther down a "Pork and Beef Center" occupying the house where the socialist Goldman family once lived. "They're Jews but they don't practice," my mother used to say of them. "Like Jesus," my father added. I followed down Victoria Street and Walworth Road, hearing sounds that were no doubt the whiskey talking in my head or the scrape of my shoes on the pavement but that came to me as voices from the past, with Eve's brightest among them, calling me to play or home for dinner. Then suddenly we were on Adeleide Road and my guide was knocking on the arched wooden door at the side of the synagogue. It was opened and I called out, "Wait a minute."

Inside, in a small vestibule that had once served as changing room for the rabbi and cantor, seven men and two teenage boys stood on a worn green carpet and addressed the holy ark. A tenth man, tall, with smooth features and gray hair—the well-groomed look of a wealthy local potentate—busied himself in showing my guide to her separate place; she was to be distinguished from us by an imaginary line that marked passage to the main body of the synagogue, which, unlit and unheated, loomed like a cathedral of gloom behind her back.

The service continued in song and prayer. I stumbled over an aluminum chair and into my place. The young woman took her coat off. She was wearing black jeans and a brightly colored knit pullover. She removed her hat and her hair fell into its fashionably cut place. Her face was open and bright. *You are wrong, Eve,* I thought. *And you too, Stewie: See how the community revives in this lovely young woman?* She opened to a page and began to chant along with the rest of our small group.

My cousin was not in the room. She must have come and gone, too cold here for her aching body. I had no doubt missed her again. The service was nearing its end, and so I waited for the last melody to fade and the prayer books to snap shut before I turned to my companions to ask after Eve, but they were already gathered around the young woman and peppering her with questions.

"A visitor?"

"From where?"

"Ah, from New York. But . . . ah, based in London, I see."

"For whom? For MTV? The rock and roll? No joking."

"Of course, Elvis Costello. We're not ignoramuses."

"The album cover? Staying with the photographer? Sure. Everybody knows her—her father was an optician down on Camden Street."

"But why here tonight? Do you, now? Weekend jaunts? Well, why not? In Italy and all? Jews everywhere, as you say."

"Debbie? You're a Debbie. Now, I have a Debbie and so does Mr. Hesselberg here."

The men gathered around Debbie as if she were speaking from a burning bush, or in some other way emanating light, an efflorescence from God's distaff side.

I exited and waited in the cold by the hedge outside the synagogue. A bright crescent moon hung mosquelike and incongruous over the temple's dome. Debbie appeared with silver-haired Mr. Stein.

"What we need," he was explaining, "is a thousand of those Russians who go to Israel. We've got a school with no students, a synagogue and a social club with no members. The only institution that's full is the old people's home."

I stepped toward them, but as I did so I heard a rip and felt the press of something cold on my arm. I had caught the sleeve of my coat on one of the railings that gated the synagogue. By the time I extricated myself the congregation had moved on into the night. I hurried back toward the river. Turning onto Harcourt

Street I saw to my surprise that once again the young woman was ahead of me, and again I followed. Her blue coat glowed in car headlights as if coated in phosphorescent paint, until I arrived outside Eve's place, where the girl disappeared and the blue revolving light on an ambulance roof replaced her.

Fundamentals

Whenever Nick Bloom, a modern, observant Jew, came to New York I would let him sleep with me, even though I knew he was married and had a family in London. I did this because, despite our disagreeing about almost everything that mattered, I found him both sexy and charming. Nick exhibited what was, to me, anyway, an irresistible combination of certain appealing physical features, nice arms and a great smile, and an ability to appear genuinely interested in my life and, more important, my work. Hardly anyone cares about art these days, not the kind that I do, anyway, which doesn't make money and still involves paint and canvases. So Nick's ability, after a couple of visits to my studio, to have a conversation about what I was doing in a way that meant something and didn't seem to be simply a prelude to sex counted for a lot.

I suppose in Nick's case the British accent contributed to his allure, and I liked to hear him talk in what I thought were "Oxford" intonations—I was wrong about that. Nick, it turned out, despite his vivid descriptions of the place, hadn't been anywhere near Oxford, or rather, he had, but only briefly in his misspent youth (before he found God) and as a salesman, not a student, purveying hashish through the college gates to, among others, friends of Bill Clinton. "I provided the joints that Clinton didn't inhale," he told me one crisp Sunday morning in Tribeca as he sat propped up on pillows in my megabed, reading the weddings in the *Times* Style section (he loved to do that: sometimes he'd cut the big one out and attach it to the fridge with a magnet). "And by the way, you don't have to inhale to get stoned. The buds on your tongue do a fine job."

I also liked fucking him, and I can give you one small moment that will explain why. On our second night together Nick was trying, in that "I'm not really trying" kind of way, to turn me on my front (I have never slept with a man who hasn't instigated some kind of acrobatics—they seem to feel obliged to show how into it and creative they are, or perhaps it's simply an attempt to demonstrate their superiority over previous lovers), and eventually I rolled over, because in sex as in politics I am not ideologically committed to conservative positions. But as I did so I said, "If you're going to do that I would like it if you held me." I have made this request before and the result has always been an awkward lunge from behind for my breasts and a kind of tree-toppling effect that I haven't particularly enjoyed. At times I have thought that, gymnastically speaking, I have been requesting the impossible. Nick, however, understood that I was asking for tenderness as a kind of counterweight to the faceless friction of coming from behind, and he managed somehow to enfold me in his long simian arms, or perhaps it was simply that he created, through his voice or the way his hands touched my skin, an aura of consideration (I don't mean to sound either Victorian or boringly pop-psych), and the result was that I felt embraced rather than screwed.

The other good thing about him was how he dealt with my looks, and I'll explain what I mean.

I once read in a magazine at the hairdresser's that above all else human beings treasure symmetry in another's face, which is something that I expressively don't have. I was born with a strabismus and next to no vision in my left eye. As a result I got teased a lot in school, first because I squinted and then because I wore an eye patch. In eighth grade I also had trouble with the art teacher, Mr. Levitan. "Alice, you're not seeing it," he used to tell me whenever we drew still lifes, which is kind of a daft thing to say to someone with no depth perception. "No," I'd reply, "I'm just not see-ing it the way you see it." Anyway, most people do a double take when they first meet me, a kind of De Niro "You talking to me?"—looking one way and pointing another. Now, by all accounts I'm an attractive woman; I have this great red hair and a Modigliani-shaped face. I'm not Kate Moss in the body, but I'm not a beanbag either. I've never had trouble getting guys. Nevertheless, I still get upset by reactions to my eyes, and, hey, how come the PC people haven't gotten on to the way that prejudice against facially challenged people like myself is embedded in the language? "You're not being straight with me," "cross," "double cross," and so on.

Back to Nick: Almost the first words that came out of his mouth when he met me were "You have beautiful eyes." Lots of women have been on the receiving end of these four words and it's a dead phrase to them, but I haven't. Later in the night (before, after, inter), I've frequently heard "You have beautiful breasts," but my eyes, those windows on the soul, get politely ignored. The thing is, Nick seemed to mean what he'd said. I didn't feel that he was handing me a line, flattering me, or even trying to seduce me with an outright lie. He looked right into my face, as if gazing at a portrait, and made an aesthetic assessment. Yay, Nick! It was moments like these that helped me put aside the awkward contradiction in his life between his beliefs and his behavior. After all, this God-fearing man who didn't ride or carry on the Sabbath was also an unashamed adulterer.

I met him in the corniest of ways, at the yogurt counter in an airport lounge. I was looking for something quite different from a British Jew with a knitted skullcap on his head and a weird problem on his hands when I found him. But fate sometimes deals a more interesting card than the one you're hoping for. Nick was on his way from London to Tel Aviv because two paintings by his long-dead grandfather Alan Bloomberg, a fairly well-respected British artist, fond of travel and best known for his conservative landscapes of exotic places—Spain, Gibraltar, Palestine—had shown up in a Jerusalem Dumpster. The newly discovered works, properly signed, dated 1922, and worth, Nick guessed, about $75,000 each, were uncharacteristically graphic and violent. To complicate matters, the canvases were accompanied by a freshly severed left hand, dyed blue from wrist to fingertips.

From the point of view of the Jerusalem police, Nick told me, there was no reason to believe the proximity of paintings to hand anything other than an odd coincidence. The blue hand was a detail, someone's grisly revenge on a local thief, and hardly worth an investigation. The paintings, however, represented big bucks. According to Nick, everyone in the Holy City was eager to learn how they had wound up in the garbage.

I was intrigued, especially because of the art connection, but I'd better backtrack a little so you get the whole picture.

In February 1995 I was in Manhattan at the movies. I had gone, like everyone else grasping at straws of beauty and meaning that endless winter, to see *Il Postino*. I was watching that weary postman push his bike up an Italian hillside when someone's watch blipped. Everybody must have heard it, but I was the only one who reacted. I threw my arms up in despair. "Stop flapping," the woman behind me said. "I can't see." Half an hour later, as the credits rolled, Mrs. Unflappable took a cell phone from her bag and dialed someone called Henry. "Long," she said. I jammed behind her in the aisle—she was still talking. "Order Chinese," she added. "I'll be there in half an hour. No MSG."

On my bus home, the kid next to me—he must have been about fifteen—opened his laptop as excitedly as I've seen some men unzip their flies, and started to play what looked like a stock market game—or maybe it was the actual stock market. I felt like weeping.

My reaction to the ubiquitous techno-fest was to put down my brushes and get into ethnobiology. I went to the Forty-second Street library and took out a stack of books. I read Jane Goodall on chimps, Diane Fossey on gorillas, and Biruté Galdikas on orangutans. Reports of the earliest forest sounds, a brachiatorial swish, or any electronically uncluttered Ur-noise or din, a diapason of calls from the canopy, were, among other things, what I was after. The other things included a general sense of deceleration. In New York, where the whole population appears to be out chasing the millennium, the air is charged. Out on the street you can hear the crackle and electric pop of progress, as if the future were falling back toward the city's eager travelers even as they pursue it.

I was hopeful of amelioration—I generally am—but reading about my writers' adventures in remote spots of Borneo and Tanzania, and the deep thinking their activities led them into, failed to calm my sense of cosmic disturbance. I began to feel that I had to visit one of the planet's last plausibly unsullied areas before it was too late. "A walk in the rain forest," Ms. Galdikas says, "is a walk into the mind of God." I wanted to take that path, preferably at a stroll.

For two weeks I spent all of my spare time seated at the kitchen table in my loft, leafing through travel mags and brochures. While I gazed at photographs of Indonesian archipelagoes or the broad zebra-filled expanses of the African savannah, ice formed in delicate lace patterns on my windows. I reviewed all the possibilities. I was tempted by Australia and even more by Costa Rica, whose rain forest, relatively small and accessible, seemed like a good one for beginners. But in the end I plumped for Africa.

Do I sound like a dilettante? I'm not. I'm serious about my work, and disciplined. I won't deny that I have some unearned money in the bank. I don't like to think of myself as a trust-fund babe, but there's no doubt that without Dad's success as a lawyer I wouldn't be in this space and getting by on two nights' teaching per week at Cooper Union. Oh, I'd still be painting—I know that from our contentious years back in the early eighties when he more or less cut me off on the unarguable grounds of bad boyfriends. "Let's see, Alice, what happens when you have to do some real work for a change," he said. I got a hellish job hand-painting T-shirts for Marshall and Marcy Hershfeld, a couple of heavy coke snorters who lived out on Long Island and owned a sweatshop in the East Village. Twice a month the cops would come and all the immigrant girls would run up on the roof. I left when the distaff member of the two vacuum noses accused me of coming on to her revolting husband. I kept one of the T-shirts I had designed: a slice of cake with a cherry on top and the words SOHO SWEETIE.

I never got to Tanzania. In the transit lounge at Heathrow my shoulder bag got stolen: passport, money, sketchpad, diary, mini-Rolodex, makeup, prescription drugs, hairbrush, novel for the plane, beeswax lip salve, everything. It took seven working days of phone calls, faxes, haggling, hassles, and traipsing back and forth from my grotty hotel in South Kensington to the U.S. Embassy in Grosvenor Square to get my life back in order.

London in February was absolutely the last place that I wanted to be. I had planned on hearing pure woodwinds or the rustle and sharp crack of boughs broken and flung down by elusive feral creatures, rain drumming on a hut rather than on the roofs of passing cars. I wanted parakeet in the shadow of Kilimanjaro, not the grays and dirty greens of another fucked-up, compu-driven city. But at least I met Nick.

The British: Unlike most Americans I know I am not particularly fond of the British, although, as I say, I find the English accent seductive, but then again I am impressed and/or delighted by almost all accents other than my own, which is standard New York. I don't find the British, or maybe I should say the English, particularly clever or witty, and their famous irony often strikes me as plain old derision and sneering, provincial nastiness masquerading as sophisticated repartee. They are also grumpy and indignant, especially in regard to requests deemed unreasonable, as, for example, mine evidently became after several hours of frustration at Heathrow. "Listen," I'd said to the customer relations guy from Virgin, "just call the fucking gate or wherever to check that my bags were taken off the plane when I didn't show up and are not at this moment on their way to Dar es Salaam." And he replied, "I will not do anything until you modify your language, madam. I am not in this job to take abuse."

Maybe I'm prejudiced. I had a brief thing with a British TV producer whom I picked up at the Edinburgh Festival about fifteen years ago when I was traveling through Europe after graduating from Pratt. He was in current affairs, and while we were together his clever friends threw a dinner party in London to which everyone had to bring his or her "current affair." It was actually my first exposure to extramarital sex (his, not mine).

Anyway, I'm getting off the point. Nick's plane to Tel Aviv was delayed by mechanical problems, so he had a freebie for one night in an airport hotel. We spent it together and had a perfectly satisfactory safe-sex one-night stand. After breakfast he gave me ten minutes on why my quest was misguided, how the sacred was to be discovered through God's holy places, Abraham's tomb in Hebron, for example, and the Bible, and Talmud, not the treetops of Africa. Then he went his way and I went mine, on into the gloom of South Kensington, and, miserably, ten days later, exhausted and depressed, back to New York.

The memory of our night of love had more or less faded (these things never go away entirely) when Nick showed up in Manhattan. A Madison Avenue dealer was interested in the salvaged Jerusalem Bloombergs. Nick had taken time off from his work—he was the "creative consultant" for a company that enhanced corporate images—to explore the possibilities of a sale. There were all kinds of issues surrounding provenance and ownership that apparently necessitated Nick's crossing the Atlantic once every couple weeks. The paintings were still in the hands of the Jerusalem police. Anyway, as I've indicated, I was happy to see him.

At the beginning of June another painting turned up, cut from its frame, rolled up, and left in a drained sesame oil vat down an alleyway in Jerusalem's Old City: a blue hand was there too, this time a right one. Now there could be no doubt that something a little out of the ordinary was going on. Nick was obliged to make another trip to Israel; he asked me if I wanted to tag along, and, like many a mistress before me, I seized the opportunity for a risk-free overseas liaison. He told me to pack at least a couple of suitcases. He planned, when he had time, to take me all over the country. In parts of the north, he said, the nights were cold even in summer.

Fundamentals

If the mind of God is the rain forest, then Jerusalem must be some other, more confused part of the deity's being—maybe God's tormented soul. All the ingredients are there for heightened spiritual experience: impressive sunsets, evocative architecture, a house of worship on every corner, the loud clash of myth and history reverberating down stony pathways once trod or flown over by David, Jesus, and Mohammed. And yet, as desert-edge omphali go, this one's jarringly hooked in to the here and now, and busted by noise. The kids are online, there's Burger King in the local mall, MTV in the front room, and streets jammed with honking traffic.

At the Laromme Hotel, the east wall windows of which face the Old City and across the gray-brown valley of Kidron, Nick had booked us, like a couple in a fifties comedy, into adjoining rooms. This seemed like an unnecessary precaution to me, but he claimed that his wife had relatives in Tel Aviv, nosy pokes who would be coming up to visit him. He couldn't take any risks.

A taste for the expedient can diminish the magic in a charmer's charms *tout suite,* but I had come a long way, and although I pretended otherwise I wasn't averse to having my own space. In fact, I was used to it. What I wasn't used to was having Nick fuck and run. His New York trips had been lazy affairs spiced by long mornings in bed. Here in Jerusalem he was off before dawn, sometimes not returning until late at night. In conversation he became abrupt and elliptical, and his lovemaking was cursory and ineffective. I decided to make the best of things, stay poolside and work on my tan.

As excuses for his bad behavior Nick repeated the myriad problems he had to face: disputed ownership of the paintings (because they were found in a municipal Dumpster, the city of Jerusalem had a claim); the business of the blue hands, regarding which, for some reason, the police desired to hear Nick's entire life story; sensation-mongering journalists; dubious art collectors; and even an old rabbi who rose from nowhere to assert before an audience of admirers and one or two local scribes that Nick's grandfather owed his yeshiva a huge unpaid debt for a portrait commission paid in advance but never fulfilled back in 1923.

On Saturday morning, which was the fourth day of our trip, Nick followed me down to breakfast at the hotel's banquet-size buffet and arrived short-tempered and indecisive.

"I don't know if I want a fucking roll," he yelled at me.

"I didn't ask you if you did," I replied.

He stormed through the double doors. I thought he'd be gone for the usual few hours, but this time he didn't come back at all. By the following morning I was apprehensive, but I certainly didn't want to assume the responsibilities of a concerned wife, so I decided to go about my business as a tourist. I bopped down the Via Dolorosa, got bored out of my mind at the Wailing Wall, and found peace and happiness in an air-conditioned room full of paintings at the Israel Museum. I even saw a Bloomberg, *The Scottish Piper in Jerusalem,* a painting even duller than its title.

Eventually the police found their way to me—eight million people had seen Nick and me going into my room together—and brought the cheerful news that Nick Bloom had been found floating facedown in Tel Aviv's River Yarkon with his hands cut off and stuffed in his pockets.

"Dyed blue?" I asked, although that wasn't at all what I intended to be the first words out of my mouth— an obsession with color is a painterly affliction.

"No," they said, "red with blood."

I sat down in a state of shock, and then I started to weep, which seemed to please everybody present. I was shaking, then shivering, and I broke out in goose bumps as I had the first time Nick touched my arm in the lobby of the Skyhotel. Two nights earlier this guy's hands had been all over me, above, behind, between, below. Now they had an independent existence sleeping with the fishes. I tried closing my eyes, but that was a disaster: Nick's stumps only got bloodier and his body bloated to Goodyear blimp size. I ran into the bathroom and threw up.

Eventually the police, two short, heavyset gentlemen in plain clothes, got me into a car and off we went, zigzagging through a cluster of limestone buildings tinged pink in the dusk. It was Friday night around six o'clock, and the streets were more or less deserted.

When we stopped at lights in the center of town I heard gunshots, but it turned out to be a woman in a dotted kerchief beating a carpet that was hung over the rail of a balcony. She got six good whacks in before the light turned green. Dust drifted around her in a nimbus of rosy light. This was a nightmare.

After four cups of coffee and three hours of interviews in a small whitewashed room near a place ominously called the Russian Compound, it became clear to Detective Yoel Lorch, a tall, heavyset blond man sporting an incongruous patriarchal beard, a white one-size-too-small wife-beater shirt, and baggy khakis, that despite my artistic talents and obvious brainpower I was something of a dip, a person who couldn't conceal a paintbrush behind an elephant.

I had told him, in the interstices between passing on everything I knew or could remember that involved Nick, about my thus-far failed effort to restore my soul by traveling outside the rubicons of millennial technology. In answer to the question "How did you meet Bloom?" I took pains to point out that I was absolutely not a New Age person or Deepak Chopra fan and that the ways of the East meant as little to me as the ways of the West. Detective Lorch replied, "But you are a Jew, no?"

In what must have seemed like a non sequitur but at the time appeared to me a logical response, I asked Detective Lorch if he was aware that cathedral architecture had its roots and inspiration in the arching canopies of the globe's great forests and the awestruck gaze of our forebears as, in some chanced-upon glade, they checked out and took in the treetops bending and swaying toward one another. The chimps at Gombe, I added by way of a QED, had been observed on rocky points, staring in reverence and amazement at the rushy cascades of a waterfall. Thus, the roots of religion, the origins of the scared, were to be found far beyond the temple walls of Congregation Temple Beth Shalom in Roslyn, New York, where I had been bat-mitzvahed in 1975. Hence, although I was undoubtedly Jewish, I wasn't all that interested in Yahweh and from what I had seen at the Wailing Wall, where the men were in a great hustle of communication, pumping the Torah up and down like a basketball trophy, while the women wandered empty-handed, Yahweh wasn't all that interested in me either.

When I was through, and after I had cried again thinking about Nick on the end of a boat hook with silt in his nostrils and used condoms dangling from his belt, Detective Lorch deemed it safe to pass on some interesting information regarding my paramour. Nick Bloom did have a wife and two kids in London, but he had been separated from them for at least three years. He *was* a "creative consultant" but in the marijuana smuggling business, not the image-enhancing one. Over the last seven years he and an American partner had been responsible for shifting a hundred tons of dope from Pakistan and Thailand, where there were fields and fields of the stuff, to London and New York, where a lot of people greatly desired to smoke it. Cops worldwide had been watching Nick since he was a child, but they couldn't pin anything on the guy. Was he in Israel to open new Middle Eastern markets? The peace treaty with Jordan, the opening up of South Africa—who knew what silken paths contemporary dope traders were mapping in their puff-smoke minds? In all likelihood Nick had been planning to use me as an unwitting courier. Someone whose suitcases (had he asked me to travel with at least two?) could be lined with illegal substances and who, if caught, would be no loss to the business. If I made it through customs I would not have my cases for long. Moreover, there was nothing to the art/hands story Nick had told me; my deceased lover had clearly owned a vivid imagination. "Severed appendages and high art do not usually go together," said Detective Lorch with a laugh. I decided not to mention Van Gogh. There was one more thing: The man I had been sleeping with was not Nick Bloom; he was Jerry Mazure. He was not an observant Jew but a Jewish con man, a master of seduction, disguise, and alias. And there was one more thing: I shouldn't be too quick to abandon Yahweh; he worked in mysterious ways and had rescued us from the idiocy of superstition and idolatry. Had I heard of "The Singing Detective"? Well, he, Yoel Lorch, was "The Religious Detective." God was his guide and mentor, through whom the truth would come out.

Whenever in the past I have been confronted with a situation that is immoderately confused or in some way overdetermined, like getting pregnant, for example, I have tended to react by heading for the nearest bar until the whole thing clarifies itself through drink. I was not pregnant now (although I have been, twice), but the feeling that whatever I chose to do next would be wrong was present in force. I could go back to the States and begin again with my paint tubes, brushes, empty canvases, and haughty disdain for the modern world, or I could stay in Jerusalem and, as they say, help the police with their inquiries. Detective Lorch, to my surprise, urged me to do the former. I wasn't a murder suspect, he said, as all my alibis checked out perfectly—my bright red hair had turned out to be an unforgettable beacon, a forest fire for the local populace—and if I remembered something new, an overheard snatch of phone conversation, an offhand remark of Jerry's ("please call him 'Nick,'" I said), anything that might give him a lead, I could call him collect from New York. He didn't think that I was in immediate danger—pot smugglers and their associates were usually nonviolent types—but it would probably be best for me to go home. If I liked, he would facilitate a plane ticket for me. I would not have to pay.

There was certainly a lot to take in and figure out, but once Nick and his drug money were out of the picture I couldn't afford to do my personal accounting at the Laromme. Neither did I wish to stay in a room where forty-eight hours earlier I had experienced a last angry fuck with a murderee.

I checked out of the Laromme without leaving a

message for Detective Lorch (I figured my hair was my forwarding address). I shouldered my canvas holdall, lifted my oversize, overweight suitcases, and headed toward the Old City, seeking the meager shade of its crenellated walls. The sun was high and hot, the straps of my bag cut into my shoulder, and the suitcase handles soon rubbed blisters into my palms. I was miserable. Taxis curb-crawled next to me and honked their horns. Sometimes the drivers or their companions leaned out and yelled, "Hey, Gingy. Where you going? Too hot to walk. Don't walk. Too much stuff." I don't know why I decided to suffer in this way (I suppose someone had to punish me for my foolishness), but I felt obliged to keep walking and give them my best *Il Postino* "schlep up the hill to Neruda" look, which, as it attempted to reflect a complex inner state combining village wisdom with a desire for sophisticated enlightenment, probably came out as a wacky stare. At any rate, around noon I wound up in East Jerusalem, where Palestinian shopkeepers snoozed on chairs in front of their stores or pulled down metal shutters and left for their afternoon siestas.

Not far from Damascus Gate I stopped in the entrance to a small hotel. In the lobby two English tourists, a lanky blond girl and her boyfriend, were arguing with the proprietor. The Brits had their guidebook out.

"It says fixed price here." The girl's voice came out in a tired whine.

"Fixed price? What fixed price? You bring me an old book. You think they know my price in London?"

"We're not from London. We're from Manchester."

"Show me that."

The girl turned to her boyfriend.

"Bad mood," she said.

There was more bickering, then raised voices and finally insults before the couple left.

I was decidedly against Brits at this moment, on account of my life having been turned upside down by one, so when I entered the lobby I tried to show their entire nation up by behaving in an extravagantly courteous manner. The hotel proprietor followed suit, and, as with lovers on their first rebound date, Mr. Nasim and I were kind and gentle with each other right through dessert, which in this case was the issue of fresh sheets.

I spent the long afternoon curled on a narrow mattress in the fetal position, perspiring, shivering feverishly, afraid to sleep, listening to the nasal call of the local muezzin and intermittently mulling my own stupidity and the complexities of trust—who's a bigger fool, the one who trusts or the one who betrays? I couldn't get too self-righteous. After all, I hadn't known Nick was separated from his wife when I hooked up with him. Eventually I slipped into some dark Kafkan dream of pursuit and punishment for something I hadn't done—jumping the turnstile on the IRT at Astor Place—but at least I was in New York.

Around seven p.m., I awoke. The sky over Jerusalem had colored up orange and gold: the local God doing his best "if you don't believe in me, take a look at this baby and think again." But instead of getting whacked by faith I got this desolate feeling of terminal loneliness (I seemed to remember reading that the apes got sad at dusk), but then, like a quick-fix miracle, Detective Lorch materialized outside my door.

He was a couple days earlier than I had expected, and maybe that's why at first I didn't recognize his voice. It was a while before I slipped the lock.

"How would you like dinner?" he asked when I finally let him in. "You've had a tough few days."

"What's your real name?" I replied.

He laughed.

"My real name is Steven Spielberg."

"OK," I said, "let's go."

Despite his unfortunate taste in undershirts (I like the muscle thing on Bruce Springsteen but hardly anybody else), Detective Lorch appeared to be a nice, trustworthy man. But then, what did I know about character? I obviously had no depth perception.

Lorch took me to a place called Mama Sophia's, where we sat in a lantern-lit garden flanked by jasmine bushes. As soon as we were settled, Lorch reached across the table and handed me my plane ticket home.

"Take it," he said. "It's the wise thing to do."

He had been thinking about me, he continued, and the endlessly duplicitous nature of men, which was something he believed I should watch out for. To help me resist future charmers like Jerry Mazure/Nick Bloom he had decided to provide me with an amulet. He laughed and produced from his pants pocket a thin necklace that displayed a small blue hand with a turquoise stone at its center. He stroked his beard and watched me as I put it on. "It's tradition," he said, "to ward off the evil eye. Many women wear them." Now here was charm from another direction, I thought, the right side of the law.

Lorch was forking a pad of eggplant ravioli into his mouth when he suddenly clutched his stomach and headed smartly for the bathroom. While he was gone the cell phone that he had left sitting by his half-empty plate emitted its thin, familiar cries for help. I picked it up and flipped it open.

"All done," the voice on the other end said, and then there was a click.

Lorch came back. Did I know, he asked me, that God had promised the Land of Israel to the Jews and that included the town of Hebron, which Abraham had purchased for four hundred shekels of silver? Was I aware that peace with the Arabs was a chimera, that the Right in Israel was always demonized, and so on and so on? I didn't feel like arguing but my silence only encouraged him. On he went, glancing back and forth from his cell phone to my unbalanced gaze. Eventually I announced that I was tired. He was reluctant to leave but in the end agreed to take me home. He suggested that we walk—the warm desert wind was God's breath sweetening His holiest place.

Lorch held my arm. I feigned tiredness so that I wouldn't have to speak. You see, I had recognized the voice on the other end of the phone, a husky British whisper that had become familiar to me through the act of love. Detective Lorch, God's lieutenant, left me at the entrance to my hotel, made sure I had entered the spin of the revolving door, then scurried into the darkness.

I called the police. Gingerly, carefully, with robots and in full protective gear, they approached the suitcases in my room, where slender lines of Semtex and thin timing devices had been set to augment the lingerie compartments. Who was going on my plane? Someone important to the peace process whose death was worth the loss of three hundred (including myself) to Nick Bloom and Detective Lorch, or the two men with their faces, accompanied by eight others, who assembled the following week in a Jerusalem courtroom to affirm their guilt with pride and yell how the God of Abraham, Isaac, and Jacob had authorized and would personally vindicate their behavior.

The day before I left Jerusalem I went to the Biblical Zoo. It was a sultry afternoon. The monkeys picked ticks from one another's hair, the great cats slept behind purple-shadowed rocks. In a narrow enclosure a camel tried to mount his mate with an awkward splay of legs and mouthy cries. I remembered reading somewhere in my anthropological texts how it was woman who had invented love. The million-year-long evolution of breasts, the shift in the position of the vagina, all that work to get man around to the front and staring into her eyes and—once that was accomplished—there it was: love, and with love, immediately, deceit.

I walked around the front of the camels to get a good look at the female. "Here," I said. And I threw her my lucky charm.

About the Author

Jonathan Wilson was born in London in 1950 and educated at the University of Essex; St. Catherine's College, Oxford; and the Hebrew University of Jerusalem. He has lived in the United States since 1976, with a four-year interlude in Jerusalem. He is the author of three works of fiction, *A Palestine Affair, The Hiding Room,* and *Schoom,* and two critical works on the novels of Saul Bellow. His stories have appeared in *The New Yorker, Ploughshares, Tikkun,* and numerous journals and anthologies including *Best American Short Stories.* His articles, essays, and reviews have appeared in the *New York Times Magazine, New York Times Book Review, Times Literary Supplement, The New Yorker, Forward, Boston Globe,* and elsewhere. He held a John Simon Guggenheim Fellowship in Fiction for 1994. He is chair of the English Department at Tufts University and lives in Newton, Massachusetts, with his wife and their two sons.